About the A

Baylea Hart is an IT Technician by day, horror writer by night and a reader everywhere in between. In 2013 she wrote, directed and edited the short horror film *Behind the Door*, which won a Top 50 spot in the Bloody Cuts 'Who's There?' competition. In October 2015 she won the Bristol Horror Writing Competition with her short story 'Jack in the Box' and had it published in the *Far Horizons* e-magazine. Her short story 'Eyes Open' was published in the 12th issue of *9 Tales Told in the Dark* in 2016.

Baylea graduated with a BA in Creative Writing from Bath Spa University and enjoys watching people grow slightly white after reading her stories.

She can be found on Twitter @bayleahart and on her website www.bayleahart.com.

CW01467722

THE LOG HOUSE

THE LOG HOUSE

BAYLEA HART

This edition first published in 2017

Unbound

6th Floor Mutual House, 70 Conduit Street, London W1S 2GF

www.unbound.com

All rights reserved
© Baylea Hart, 2017

The right of Baylea Hart to be identified as the author of this work has been
asserted in accordance with Section 77 of the Copyright, Designs and
Patents Act 1988. No part of this publication may be copied, reproduced,
stored in a retrieval system, or transmitted, in any form or by any means
without the prior permission of the publisher, nor be otherwise circulated in
any form of binding or cover other than that in which it is published and
without a similar condition being imposed on the subsequent purchaser.

ISBN (eBook): 978-1911586470
ISBN (Paperback): 978-1911586463

Design by Mecob

Cover image:

© Picture Library

To my family,
for giving me Stephen King books to read as a child.
This is all your fault.

Dear Reader,

The book you are holding came about in a rather different way to most others. It was funded directly by readers through a new website: Unbound.

Unbound is the creation of three writers. We started the company because we believed there had to be a better deal for both writers and readers. On the Unbound website, authors share the ideas for the books they want to write directly with readers. If enough of you support the book by pledging for it in advance, we produce a beautifully bound special subscribers' edition and distribute a regular edition and e-book wherever books are sold, in shops and online.

This new way of publishing is actually a very old idea (Samuel Johnson funded his dictionary this way). We're just using the internet to build each writer a network of patrons. Here, at the back of this book, you'll find the names of all the people who made it happen.

Publishing in this way means readers are no longer just passive consumers of the books they buy, and authors are free to write the books they really want. They get a much fairer return too – half the profits their books generate, rather than a tiny percentage of the cover price.

If you're not yet a subscriber, we hope that you'll want to join our publishing revolution and have your name listed in one of our books in the future. To get you started, here is a £5 discount on your first pledge. Just visit unbound.com, make your pledge and type LOGHOUSE17 in the promo code box when you check out.

Thank you for your support,

Dan, Justin and John
Founders, Unbound

Super Patrons

Ben Allen
Jack Austin
Will Dean
Penny Evans
Jack Evans
Nathan Farajian
Julie Hart
Graham Hart
Mitchell Hart
Carolyn Hassan
Paul Holbrook
Small Town Horror
Robert Iwataki
Markus mini Johansson
Dan Kieran
Ewan Lawrie
Sophie Marie Mills
John Mitchinson
Andy Morgo
Christine Murphy
Justin Pollard
Sophie Pratt
Jonathan Price
Jonathan Price
Pete Sutton
Wayne Turner
Janine Tweedie
Mark Waddoups
Nan
Balthazar

With grateful thanks to Graham Hart, Jack Austin and Steve Kelsey, who helped make this book happen.

The woods are lovely, dark and deep,
But I have promises to keep,
And miles to go before I sleep,
And miles to go before I sleep.

—Robert Frost, 'Stopping by Woods on a Snowy Evening'

Before #1

Penny pressed the thick cardboard sheet against the window, breathing in its damp musk. She traced the edge of the board with gentle fingertips, scrutinising every corner for the slightest trace of light. She did this three times, pushing the sheet firmly when she noticed a corner slightly raised, or a small pocket of air beneath its surface.

After every new movement, she checked the sheet again. Only when she was sure that the window was completely covered did she dare step out from behind the thick, sun-stained curtains and into the room behind her.

Golden light, faint and flickering, beckoned her to the opposite side of the room. She walked over to it, stopping when the air became warm and tinged with the smell of smoke. With a fluid motion that came from years of practice, Penny leaned forward, grasped the two leather straps that jutted out of the wall in front of her and pulled.

Stone scraped against stone. Penny dragged the brick fireguard to one side, leaning it against the rest of the wall, and crouched down to examine the embers it had obscured. She threw a log onto the flames, and poked around with a twisted metal skewer until the log had started to char.

She stood.

Stretched.

The fire grew stronger, bringing life to the room around her. A room she loved, despite the crumbling wallpaper and battered, wooden floor. Beside her, a crooked wardrobe leaned into the wall. Penny had ripped its doors off many years ago, and now it looked much like a waiting mouth with a small selection of worn, faded clothing visible in the dimness.

The only other functional piece of furniture was a small double bed, pressed up against the far wall. Blankets were piled upon it, the colour of stale yellowed cream, plush and thick for the cold winters.

Inside the bed lay a boy of around five years.

His thin, pale face was almost entirely obscured by the fabric that surrounded him, and was very nearly the same colour. Penny walked over to the bed, and knelt beside it, tugging at the blankets around the boy to create some sort of order. Her shadow danced on the wall behind her, twitching and writhing.

The boy sank further into the bed.

'Mama.' His voice was barely audible above the sound of rustling fabric.

'Hush, it's bed time,' said Penny.

'I'm scared.'

'Don't be silly. There's nothing to be scared of here. Go to sleep.'

'Don't go.'

'Go to sleep.'

Penny pulled the blankets away from the boy's face and tucked them into what had once been a mattress. He struggled beneath the weight, wriggling awkwardly but unable to move much beyond stretching out his legs. He looked up at Penny, his eyes wet and flickering in the light.

He has such sad eyes, she thought.

'Goodnight,' Penny said. The boy sniffed and looked away.

'Night,' he said softly.

Penny pinched his cheek, but said nothing else. She rose to her feet, watching as his eyes closed and, after a few moments, his face softened and relaxed.

His chest rose and fell. Slow and heavy. Penny checked the room a final time making sure that all light was safely locked within, and then crept out of the room, leaving the boy to the soft glow of the fire and the door ever so slightly ajar behind her.

She walked down the long hallway towards the dining room, praying she would have time to clear the remains of the evening meal before lights out. She walked quickly, head down, listening closely to the soft padding of her footsteps. Doorways loomed all around her, bedrooms following bedrooms. Some doors were open, and fellow house-dwellers waved politely as she passed. She smiled in return, thankful for friendly faces instead of locks and doorknobs. Each closed door radiated an invisible pressure that thrummed in her skull, and she raced past them when she was sure no one could see.

As she turned the corner at the end of the corridor, Penny sensed eyes upon her.

She scowled and quickened her pace, shadows warping as she moved. The hair on her arms prickled as she heard something shuffle in the darkness.

An echo of a footstep.

Not much farther. She only had to get to the dining room and she would be safe.

Penny threw up her chin and glared at the air in front of her.

A cold hand fell upon her shoulder.

Penny jumped and wheeled around, heart hammering and arms raised to defend herself. A thin woman was lurking in the shadows, her eyes cold and distant.

'Christ, Mary,' Penny said.

The other woman said nothing.

Penny lowered her arms and huffed in frustration, her cheeks warm with embarrassment. It wasn't like her to be spooked that easily.

'Well?' Penny said, after several moments had passed. 'What is it?'

Mary blinked.

'Why can't you be more gentle with him? He's only a child.'

Penny scowled. Mary had been watching her again.

'Like you know anything about treating children gently,' she said.

'You need to be kinder to him.'

'And you need to stay out of my way.'

Penny turned and began to walk once more, but no matter how quickly she moved she couldn't shake the other woman. Penny stopped again, hands on her hips, twisting her neck to glare at Mary.

'Shadows suit you, you know,' Penny said. 'Rats like the dark, I hear. Why don't you go skulk back into whatever hole you crawled out of? I don't have time to put up with you tonight.'

'He's a child. You need to be kinder to him. You know that. If other people saw the way you treat him, they'd—'

'I treat him just fine.'

'No. You don't.'

Mary's voice, flat and generally unremarkable, made Penny's

stomach clench. It was the same voice she heard in the depths of her dreams.

I can't open the door, it said. *I can't open the door.*

Penny smiled at the woman, baring her teeth.

'It's none of your business how I treat my son.'

'It's everyone's business.'

'Not yours. You have no say in anything that happens in my life. Now, are we done?'

Mary tightened her lips until they became a thin, white line. A gash in her face. She took a breath, and Penny watched her shoulders tremble.

'No. No, we're… Look, this has gone on for too long. This fighting isn't good for either of us. We need to talk.'

'We're talking now, and I'm already sick of it.'

'Not here. Outside. Will you come?'

Penny scoffed and stared down at Mary, waiting for her to fall apart under the weight of her gaze, as she usually did when faced with such direct confrontation.

Mary did not falter. She held her ground, chin raised, eyes watery and set like steel. Penny's cheeks grew hot again, and, to her surprise, she was the one to break the silence.

'The sun is setting,' Penny said. 'They'll be locking the doors soon, and then we'll be stuck outside 'til morning. Is that what you want?'

'It won't take long.'

'And what if there's something else out there? They see better in the dark, and you of all people know they sometimes come near the house. What exactly is so important that we should risk our lives instead of waiting until morning?'

Mary looked down and rubbed her hands together.

'In the morning you'll have some new excuse to ignore me. If we don't do this now, we never will. You know that.'

'Then we can talk here.'

'No,' Mary cried. 'We can't. I… I want us to finish this where it started. Outside, in the place where he…' She swallowed. 'Where we last saw him. Please, Penny. All I want is to put all this behind us. Lock it away. But it has to be *there*. Will you come?'

Penny's heart fluttered.

'Give me one good reason why I should.'

Mary's eyes locked onto Penny's.

'If you come, whether we make amends or not, I promise I will never speak to you or your son again. Not if you don't want me to. Just let me say what I need to. Please.'

Penny bit her lip. Mary was lying, obviously lying, but if there was even the slightest chance... She clenched her fists, digging her nails into the skin.

'You promise you'll leave us both alone? Leave *him* alone?'

'I promise. Will you come?'

Mary's gaze was frantic, but not uncertain. Perhaps she really wanted to be forgiven, after all this time. There was no chance of that happening, not now or ever, but that was the least of Penny's concerns at the moment. If there was even the smallest chance of getting Mary out of her son's life, Penny would move mountains.

She folded her arms across her chest.

'Will it take long? I need to be back inside before the sun sets. If I'm not in bed by morning *my son* will worry.'

Mary flinched.

'No,' she said. 'It won't take long.'

Penny followed Mary out of the house and into the stillness of the evening air. The sun had already started to vanish behind the surrounding forest and shadows were crawling their way out of the trees and up towards the house. It was unnatural, being outside so close to sunset. Every movement made Penny flinch, no matter how small or innocent it seemed. The autumn breeze, a premonition of winter, tousled her hair and licked at her neck. She wrapped her arms around herself, wishing she had picked up her jumper.

Mary moved away from the house and, to Penny's surprise, turned left when she should have turned right. They moved further and further from the place Penny had been expecting, until they eventually came upon the river, a gurgling wall that separated the house from the deep, thick forest that lay behind.

Mary stopped at the water's edge but did not turn around.

The air hummed and whispered.

'Why are we here?' Penny's initial suspicion was growing. Her eyes darted from Mary to the house.

This wasn't right. How quickly could she make it back?

'I need to show you something first.'

'Show me what? There's nothing here. Damn it, it's almost dark. I knew this was a bad idea. They'll be locking the doors soon and then what will we do? What the hell are you up to?'

'Nothing. I just need to show you this before we talk. It's important, I promise. I just need to go and get it.'

'I should never have—'

'It won't take long,' said Mary. 'Just… wait there.'

There was no time for Penny to stop her. Mary had scurried off before she could even think about calling out. Penny huffed instead, watching Mary dart into the shrubbery that marked the forest edge.

She sighed.

How could she have been so stupid? It had been such an obvious lie, a ploy to get Penny to stand outside in the cold and the dark. Vulnerable. Was she really so desperate to be rid of Mary that she would disregard all common sense? That was not how she had been raised. Mary was likely heading back to the house already, laughing at the thought of leaving her shivering in the sunset.

Locking the door behind her.

She did have a nasty habit of locking doors.

Penny clenched her fists.

She really was stupid.

Damn it.

No, it didn't matter.

Get up, brush off, move on.

She glared at the trees, turned her back to them and walked in the direction she had come.

The ground squelched as she moved.

It wasn't far to the house. She would be back before the doors were locked, and, if she was lucky, Mary might not have gone back already. If Penny really hurried, Mary might even be left outside. That would be nice.

Penny smiled and then stopped.

Frowned.

Something moved behind her, flickered in the corner of her eye.

Something fast.

She held her breath and listened.

Stared about her.

The wind ran fingers down her spine.

Penny's skin began to itch, but she refused to give in to the swell of panic. This was one of Mary's tricks; she could feel it in her core. Mary was still out there somewhere, she had to be, watching from the darkness like she always did.

Watching her.

Penny pushed her chin up and glared at the nothingness in front of her.

Ignored the soft pattering sounds that made her hair stand on end.

This was nothing, she told herself. She had been through worse than this. Mary had put her through worse.

Doors in her mind.

There was a heavy thud behind her.

A rattling hiss.

Wind whistled past her ear.

Screams. Hers, his.

A deep, nauseating pressure at the base of her skull.

Fading light.

A flash of white.

Then there was nothing at all.

Chapter One

She heard the rushing of water first, like blood roaring in her ears.

Beyond that, Penny heard the faint murmur of leaves.

It was almost like she was outside. How funny.

A gentle breeze brushed her face, bringing with it the smell of dirt and greenery, sour and delicious. She was aware of something wet against the back of her head, as if she were lying in a puddle.

Had there been a leak in the night?

Her eyes were closed. She couldn't see.

The roof was old. It might have been damaged. She would need to tell the elders later.

Penny lifted her head away from the dampness, moved her body forward slightly, and then allowed her head to fall back onto what should have been her pillow. Instead, it collided with something solid.

Lightning crackled at the base of her skull and Penny cried out as pain radiated down her body. She sat up, awake now, shivering with shock and nausea, her hands desperately reaching out for her head, but as she moved the world lurched around her.

Disorientated, dizzy, she fell onto her side, back to the hard surface. She clung to it, praying for the world to steady itself as she moved and swayed. Her breath slowed. Something wet touched her cheek. It pushed itself against her skin and rolled down the length of her face.

She froze and the fog in her mind cleared.

Penny grew aware of a cool light beyond her eyelids, which she realised she still hadn't opened. The scent of water, entwined with the green smell she had first recognised, became overwhelming. Her stomach churned.

The murmuring was too loud.

She was dizzy.

It was too bright. Too fresh. Too much.

It wasn't right.

Penny took three deep breaths and clenched her fists until she could feel dots of pain against her palm. She didn't want to open her eyes and confirm her fears, but they were already starting to sting with the tears that threatened to fall.

A bird cawed.

Penny moaned and forced her eyes open.

It was a beautiful autumn day – the perfect weather to spend outdoors splayed out on the grass with a threadbare blanket and a cool mug of water. Sunlight caressed trees of green, red and purple as Penny drifted below them. She turned her head to one side, and sprays of foam splattered against her face, conjured by the river she found herself floating on.

The river that had brought death to so many in the house.

Penny held back a scream.

How had she got here? She couldn't have been sent away. Not without a trial or a vote or... something. It just didn't happen.

This was unheard of.

Impossible.

Penny wiped sweat from her forehead with a hand that trembled uncontrollably. The movement rocked whatever makeshift boat she was lying on, causing it to plunge into the water. She cried out, shuffling back without thinking. The boat lurched in the opposite direction, the river rushing up to meet her face.

Calm down. Think. Don't just react.

Start small, Pen. Then work your way up.

She needed to stop the boat from rocking before she tumbled into the water. Penny rolled herself to the centre, taking deep breaths as she steadied herself. The boat moved back and forth, but slower now.

It was beginning to calm.

Good.

Next step.

She needed to work out what was happening, and how to get onto dry land. Penny grabbed her arm and pinched until the bare skin grew pink and her mind focused purely on the pain. She exhaled slowly and then looked around, her body barely moving at all in order to not upset whatever she was floating on.

Her arm snaked slowly around the perimeter of her body, scanning the area with nails and skin. It seemed she was floating in a small, rectangular, wooden piece of furniture. Not a boat, not in the traditional sense, but similar. It was large enough for her to fit while lying down, with walls about as high as her chest when she did so. It was wide enough for Penny to roll slightly, but only as far as her elbows. Something small and hard dug into her left hip, and when she moved her hands over to the object she found a peg pushed deep into the wooden walls around her. Like something that would hold up a shelf.

She was in a bookcase. Probably one from the collection stored in the basement as spare firewood, not tended to for years. The thin, cardboard back she lay on was becoming damp at an alarming rate. It sagged beneath Penny's weight, dipping into the water. There was no telling how much longer it would last. She could have been floating for hours already.

'It's going to sink,' she whispered to herself. 'It's going to sink. It's going to sink.'

In her memories, a warm hand wiped a tear from her face.

Get up, brush off, move on.

Penny reached for the throbbing lump at the back of her head, grazing it with a feather-light touch. She winced, scowled, and then pushed her fingers into the wound. She dug into the exposed flesh as it blazed with pain.

It must have been Mary. All these years, and she couldn't even face Penny as she stabbed the knife into her back.

How dare she attack and set her adrift like this? Was she hoping Penny would die out in the unknown? Just crawl into a hole and wait for the dark? For those… things to finish her off?

Penny was no coward. No weakling. She would claw her way back home on her hands and knees. Through mud and blood, forest and hill. Then she would show Mary how to kill someone properly. First, though, she needed to find a way off her ridiculous excuse for a boat before it sank.

Penny reached down into the water and started to paddle, pushing against the current with as much impact as a fly in a hurricane. Her arms strained and glistened as wave upon wave crashed against them. She was beginning to see why no one had ever returned once they were sent away.

Not important. Keep going.

She could risk entering the river. If it were shallow enough for her feet to touch the ground she would be fine, but the murky water made it impossible to gauge the depth. Penny had stopped swimming after her father died, and if the river was as deep as she feared, she would be left to the mercy of the waves. She wasn't confident she could make it.

There was nothing to do but paddle onward.

Penny slashed at the water, frantic; a hair's breadth from crying out in frustration as the river dragged her along without hesitation.

Her knuckles scraped along rock, and she pulled her hand to her chest, hissing in pain. Her heart leapt.

Before she had time to weigh up the decision, she threw both arms out into the water, waving them around beneath the surface.

The boat lurched and continued to move.

There wasn't much time. If she didn't find the rock immediately, it would be gone.

Her chest heaved, water sprayed into her eyes. She couldn't see. What if she had missed her chance?

Breathe.

It was still there. It had to be.

She cried out, screaming at the water as something cool and solid slipped beneath her fingertips. She scrambled for purchase, her nails snapping as they scratched against rock. Her hands brushed against a sharp crevice and she dug into it, wrapping her thumbs around a protruding lump of stone.

The boat continued to move. To pull. It moved beneath her, sliding along her legs until only her feet held it in place. For an awful moment she could see the boat slipping away completely, casting her down into the raging river.

She would be dragged away. She was going to slip.

Penny growled and pulled her body closer to the rock. The boat wobbled and then came to a sudden stop.

Penny grinned, panting, but only for a flicker of a moment.

The current was much stronger than she had expected. Her arms started to tremble with the force of the river pushing against her, arched over it like a human bridge. Her fingers began to slip.

Penny looked up. The shore was still too far for her to reach, a sharp incline of rock and roots. But there were more rocks nearby, and one was very close. Not quite close enough to reach from where she was, but close. If she could just get herself a little nearer, move the boat a little further, she might be able to make it. Then she could hop from rock to rock until she reached the river's edge.

It was a bad idea, but any idea was better than staying still.

She dug her hands deeper into the rock and pulled her body, and the boat, towards her. Her knees bent. The boat inched closer, enough to slide her knees back to safety, and then clunked loudly as it slammed into rock.

Straining, sweating, hair glued to her forehead, Penny slowly began to move around the rock. Her arms trembled and her eyes stung.

In front of her, a small grey stone peaked from below the water's surface. Penny inched closer, dragging the boat until the rock appeared to be within reach. She stopped. She had gone as far as she could. Now all she had to do was let go.

Penny stared at the rock. It seemed so far away. If the boat was in the wrong place, she'd drift right past before she could even think to grab hold.

She dug her nails deeper into the crevice, took a breath, and then she let go.

The boat lurched beneath her, moving far too quickly. Her legs, still in the bookcase, twisted painfully and Penny's whole body turned until she was staring at the sky. She tried to spin back to where she had been, stretching out her arms to grab at the rock before the river took her.

Her face hit the water, and then the world was upside down.

Penny gasped as she plunged deeper into the glacial river, but inhaled water instead of air. It forced itself into her throat and chest, clawing its way into her lungs. She coughed, sucking in more river.

It streamed in through her nose. Burned her eyes.

She spun below the surface, dizzy, unable to orientate herself. She pushed in any direction she could, arms and legs flailing.

A warm, smoky voice seeped into her thoughts, telling her to kick her legs. That was all she had to do. Just keep kicking.

Penny kicked.

She kicked against the current, chest burning. She kicked her way towards the light. Finally, she broke the surface, coughing and spluttering, but the river pulled her under before she could regain her breath. Before she could think.

Her back collided with something solid. She turned and thrashed around, desperate for anything to which she could anchor herself.

Rock slipped beneath her frantic hands.

She was running out of air.

Her fingertips grazed over a hint of rough stone, and then a large chunk of it. Penny grabbed it, forcing her hands inside any crack she could find. Secure, but losing consciousness, she forced her eyes open and began pulling herself up the rock. Hoping she was heading towards the surface.

To air.

Her vision grew hazy, and her arms screamed with pain as she hauled herself upwards.

Penny found the surface and drank in the air.

She continued crawling up the rock until she was strewn across it, clinging to it like a child, shaking and coughing as she vomited up the water inside her. Still fighting the current even now.

When her heaves subsided she looked around, reluctant to move her head more than a minuscule amount from its position against the stone. There was another rock a few metres away, within arm's reach. So close.

From there she would be able to reach the shore.

Water whipped at her face as she stretched out an arm, and just as quickly pulled it back. She couldn't reach the second rock. Not without letting go of the first. Penny swore beneath her breath.

She stretched out again, this time slightly extending the arm that kept her secure against the rock.

Just a little more.

Just a little closer.

Penny roared and then let go completely.

Her arm found the second rock easily and Penny scrambled onto it, grunting.

She looked up. Above her was a mass of tree roots sticking out of the ground like long, white fingers and cascading down until they met the water's surface. Penny grabbed the nearest one she could see that looked as though it could hold her weight and then pulled. Dirty, bloody, angry, Penny crawled up tree roots until they became the trees themselves. Her fingernails, thick with mud, clawed into the ground as she hauled herself over the edge and onto the flat forest floor.

She rolled onto her back and lay flat against the grass.

Her chest heaved.

She didn't even have the energy to cry.

Penny stared at the claw-like tree root, her chest rising and falling with each heavy breath. She watched the light upon it change, until shadows were all there were.

Her heart was racing.

Her head was pounding.

The sun was beginning to set.

She had stayed in one place for too long. She was out in the open here. Exposed. Penny needed to plan. Needed to keep moving, to find somewhere safe to hide from the encroaching darkness and the creatures that lurked within, but she had no energy left to summon and could only stare, aware of a distant dripping and the roar of the river below.

It was her own fault, really. The others may not have believed Mary had it in her, but Penny had known better.

Poor, lonely Mary.

She had always been miserable and argumentative; picking fights about rations or the decay of the house. It had got worse after Penny's son was born. Mary had become jealous and bitter. But nobody ever thought of her as vindictive. Nobody ever looked at her and saw what she was really capable of.

No one except Penny.

She shouldn't have let her guard down. All those years of peace had made her soft. Penny had watched Mary sulk in dark rooms with her insect-like husband, trying to forget what she had done, no doubt. But Mary never made her move. Never did anything to make Penny suspect. Penny didn't even go near Mary anymore. Not now she had her son. What had she done to deserve this sudden violence?

She'd done nothing.

It should be Mary, sopping wet and panting on the grass, not her.

Penny's brow furrowed as she thought back to the evening before. Mary had been watching her as she'd put her son to bed.

'It's everyone's business,' she had said.

She had always been watching them, hadn't she? Lurking in the shadows like a spider. Her eyes glinting whenever the boy smiled, like a predator waiting for its chance to strike.

Penny dug her fingernails deep into the dirt.

Mary was a predator, wasn't she?

Mary wanted to steal her child, her son. Tear him from her arms. Mary had exiled her, sent her to her death, in order to take the only thing Penny had left in the whole world.

Penny rolled onto her side, then up onto her belly, her knees and finally her feet. Her ankles gave way as she stood, and Penny wobbled, grasping a tree to stop herself from falling. Speckles danced in her vision like dust mites and her stomach cramped and gurgled.

The light in the forest had faded almost entirely; it wouldn't be long until sunset. By then, she would have missed an entire day's worth of rations. She needed to find food before anything else, and then shelter. Somewhere to hide from the cold evening while she worked out how she would get home.

Because she would get home.

And she would take her son *back*.

Penny took a step forward, testing her ankles. When the earth remained firm under her feet, she took a breath, and walked into the darkness of the trees, so unlike the forest surrounding the house.

Instead of the pretty, sentry-like trees she was used to, this forest was thick with roots and brambles, the reddening sun above hidden by a plush blanket of leaves. It was like pushing into the wind, branches catching on the holes in her shirt and pulling at her ankles. She slipped and stumbled around, hissing as she stubbed a toe that she only just realised was bare.

'Damn it,' she muttered, as a sharp twig scratched the ball of her foot. She stopped to clutch at it when a large crash, like a falling tree, echoed around her.

Penny froze, rooted to the earth, and listened to the sound of her boat hitting something large, and seemingly from a great height.

A waterfall.

That couldn't be possible. There was only one waterfall known to the house, and it was far away. She couldn't be that far from home. Deep into the outside world.

The sound reverberated for several seconds, seconds that dragged on for aeons. Penny barely dared to breathe as realisation dawned on her.

There was no light here.

Shadows everywhere.

Why had she entered the forest?

Why had she been so *stupid*?

They could find her here.

See her.

The sound would draw them.

She needed to hide.

To get away.

How had she forgotten what was out there? How had she forgotten where she was?

She had a choice, but no time to make it.

She could stay and hide and hope that the sunlight was strong enough to mask her presence, hope that the snippets of rumours and tales she had heard would turn out to be true.

Or she could run, run as far and as fast as she could.

Stay or run.

Stay or run.

Penny ran.

Chapter Two

Penny realised her mistake as soon as her foot hit the ground, but by that time the second foot was already in motion, and then it was too late to turn back.

She was never going to be able to run in this forest. The very branches themselves seemed to work against her, grabbing at her clothes with spindly, crooked fingers. She hopped over brambles high enough that they scratched at her cheek. Pushed her way through grass that grazed her bare shins. She didn't know which direction to go – the darkness of the forest was just as deadly as the alluring sparkle of the river.

Just get away from the noise, said the voice in her head. *Nothing else matters.*

She didn't care about losing sight of the river; that was a problem for later. What she cared about was the faint rustling behind her, getting ever closer and faster as the forest grew darker.

She did not look around to see what it was. She didn't need to.

Penny's breath caught in her chest, and she gasped noisily for air. Her feet thumped against the ground. A regular rhythm.

Like the knocking of a door.

The beating of her heart.

A scream in the darkness.

She was being too loud. It would hear her.

Damn it, run faster.

To her right, through a thistle bush, she could see a crooked tree, limbs bowed low enough she might be able to reach them. Penny swerved towards it and pushed through the painful plant as it scratched her skin.

She was bleeding, and the droplets ran down her arms as she wrapped them around a low branch and pulled herself up into the tree. Her feet scrambled against bark, toes stretched and searching. She managed to rest one foot on the trunk for a fraction of a second before it slipped, catching a sharp, snapped branch on its way down. Penny bit down on her tongue to stop herself from crying and reached up to the branch once again.

She pulled, her arms quivering. Her toes brushed against a small knot on the trunk, just wide enough to balance herself. She paused, took a breath, and reached for the next branch. Then the next. Up and up, Penny climbed much higher than seemed safe, and then further still. When the trunk started to sway beneath her weight, she wrapped her legs and arms around it.

She closed her eyes.

Breathed.

For a moment, Penny thought she had escaped.

Had she overreacted?

Perhaps the woods were safe now, after all these years. Perhaps it hadn't heard her. Hadn't followed.

And then came the silence.

Every animal and every bird. Every insect, every leaf on every tree, even the wind itself – it all fell still.

Watch for the silence, said the voice in her head. *It's the only warning you'll get.*

A small bead of sweat trickled down Penny's back, curling around to her waist. She could smell earth and bark.

The tree swayed.

Back and forth.

Penny tried to focus on her breath but the more she did, the more it caught in her chest. Her body throbbed in fear and pain as she tried harder and harder to force the air into her lungs. She was being too loud. Moving too much.

It would hear. It would see. It would find her.

There was a shuffle of leaves and a snap of a twig below. Penny drew herself closer to the trunk, hoping to sink inside it. Sharp edges of bark dug into her skin.

Another snap. Then a long, slow, deliberate scraping noise. A horrible scratching with such strength behind it that the tree shivered beneath her.

Penny bit her lip, tearing at the skin until she could taste blood on her tongue.

A sound from below, like a sigh, broken and distorted.

'Haaaaa.'

Her world shattered.

Not that noise. Not again. She couldn't hear it again.

Doors slammed behind her closed eyes.

A man screamed.

She trembled.

Mary's voice, full of regret.

Mary.

Penny dug her nails into the tree bark and furrowed her brow.

Mary had put her through this. Mary had done this to her. Mary had forced her into her nightmares and locked the door. Mary had done it all.

Get up, brush off, move on.

Penny's breath became even and slow. Her heartbeat slowed.

She listened as the thing below her finished its scratching, and remained still as the shuffling grew quieter. She did not move, even when she stopped hearing the shuffling entirely. Only when the birds began to sing, and the breeze raked itself through her hair, did she unwrap herself from the tree and slide down to the ground. She dropped herself from a branch and landed with all her weight on her feet. Her legs were stiff, and her left foot throbbed from the impact of the ground, sending pain radiating through her leg. Penny sank to the floor, clutching her foot and pulling it towards her.

She was bleeding. Heavily.

She looked over her shoulder, into the trees. It was safe, but it wouldn't be for long.

Wincing, she tried to clean the wound but her hands left more dirt than they removed. She tried to tear part of her shirt but the fabric wouldn't give. She swore under her breath and pulled her shirt over her head. Penny shivered against the wind and began to wipe at the blood and dirt, cleaning her foot as best as she could. She wrapped the wet shirt around her wound, tying it together with the sleeves. She breathed, slow and steady, and pushed herself up. The lumpy bandage made it difficult to stand, but it was better than bleeding all over the forest floor. Those monsters weren't the only things in the forest capable of killing her, after all.

Exhausted, Penny leaned back against the tree trunk, pushing her hair out of her face. A single wet strand flopped back against her forehead, dripping onto her nose. Her stomach cramped and she winced, pressing her hands into her stomach as if to calm it. Across her skin were the harsh pink scars that had remained after her pregnancy. The miracle pregnancy, they had called it. The first child to be born in twenty-seven years, and the very first boy to be born at all. The first… unaltered boy, anyway.

Penny stroked the lines with a gentle touch.

Her child, her son, was back at the house. No doubt Mary was already digging her claws into him, just like she had always wanted. Penny had seen the hunger in her eyes, though couldn't have said what it meant until now. She had seen it every time she walked with her son hand and hand, every time they sat down for meals together. Not to mention the incident that day by the river that still sent waves of rage pulsing through her even now.

Penny was his mother.

He was hers.

And she was not about to let Mary take him from her too.

She would make sure of it.

She pushed her back against the tree, using it to propel herself forward, but as she moved her hair became caught in a crevice of the trunk. Her eyes watered as her hair threatened to tear from her scalp, and Penny's hand shot up to stop it from pulling. She turned to free herself and the strands of hair in her hand fell from her grasp.

Penny stared at the tree in horror.

Carved into the trunk as if it were butter, were four long scratch marks, each line as deep as the length of a finger.

A child's finger.

Penny stumbled backward.

Her hair ripped and broke away from her scalp. She didn't notice. Instead, she turned her back to the tree and limped away without a second thought. She didn't want to be in this place any longer.

She did not look back.

Penny's father had walked her through the basics of survival from the moment she could speak. It was a lesson everyone had to learn eventually, whether they were chosen to participate in the annual foraging trips or not. Penny's father, as luck would have it, was chosen quite often, which meant he had a wealth of knowledge to give. They would spend afternoons together, her father pointing to various edible shrubs, or ideal places to hide from watchful eyes. She remembered vividly the night he described the creatures.

'Once it goes quiet,' he had said, resting his hand upon her head, 'hide yourself away and don't even think about moving until the sounds come back. Especially not in the dark. They see better in the dark.'

He had leaned down then, staring at her with those bright blue eyes she loved so much.

'Don't ever let one get close to you, Pen. Do you hear me? That's the most important thing. Once it can grab you, it's over.'

He'd gone back to talking of trees and animals afterwards. Penny couldn't remember much of that, but the bits and pieces she could gather from her mind were enough to form the basis of a plan.

Step one was to find shelter. The day was fading quickly, and more than anything right now, Penny needed somewhere to hide. The next step would be to make her way back to the river. She would need water to survive, and once she got to the river, she would be able to follow it back up through the forest. From what she could remember from her father's stories, after some time the river would rise up into the hill, and the hill gradually became rockier and barren until it finally reached the house. It would be a bit of a climb, but she knew she would be fine up until she reached the bridge. Then everything would depend on factors outside of her control. She would not be able to reach the house without the bridge, and she would not be able to cross the bridge if there was any sign of a frost between now and then. It had been a warm summer, so the bridge should still be there for at least another few weeks. Sometimes they even left it longer, if they could. Penny didn't see the point of removing the bridge at all. Those things didn't know where the house was; they hadn't been near in years.

She shuddered.

Ignored the memories.

River, bridge and then house.

She'd been close to the waterfall, but surely it wouldn't take her longer than a week to get back. Then, once she reached the house, she would head straight to her son, to Mary, and drag the boy back out of her arms. She would seize Mary by her thin, dull, brown hair and drag her kicking and screaming to the river.

She wouldn't toss her in a boat, or abandon her in the forest. Penny wasn't a coward.

She would hold her head under the water until she drowned. Or, she could lock her inside the log house.

Yes, that way would be better. More fitting.

But that was a thought for later. Before any of that, she needed to eat.

If only she knew where to start.

Penny, not knowing what else to do, threw her head back and stared at the canopy above her. Fruit would be her best bet, and the number of trees surely meant at least one would have something edible growing. She had never worked with the crop gatherers – she had been too precious for that, and the elders didn't want to risk anything after what had happened to her mother. But Penny had often seen workers climbing trees during autumn, plucking fruit and throwing them into baskets. It was the right time of year. If they could do it, why couldn't she?

She turned on the spot. The last of the sunlight was trickling through the canopy, and fading fast. Penny followed the snaking branches with her eyes as they intertwined. She could not see any fruit, or anything else edible for that matter. Penny began to walk carefully and quietly, scanning every branch she could make out while jumping at even the slightest rustle of leaves behind her.

Nothing.

Her stomach rumbled and churned.

She bent over, clutching a nearby trunk to steady herself, and swallowed the vomit creeping up her throat. A cold evening breeze washed over her and she shivered. Her thin vest, ripped and wet, clung to her skin.

The nausea passed, and Penny stood upright, rubbing her arms to dispel the cold. As she did, a small shadow darted through the sky and into a nearby tree. Penny flinched, covering her head with her arms against the unknown danger. When she came to no immediate harm, she slowly built up her courage and peeked around her arm to stare at the tree before her.

A small brown bird hopped along a broken branch, tilting its head, as if confused at Penny's presence. When she didn't move it flew to the ground and bounced over to her, head twitching left and right. Penny watched it, unblinking. The bird's brown eyes locked onto hers. They watched each other, and Penny dared not move in case she frightened the creature away. She wanted it to flit closer. Wanted it to come and investigate the strange creature that stood in front of it.

Closer.

She just needed it to come a little closer.

Penny had visions of a small fire, the light hidden by careful rock placement. A small bird on a sharp branch roasting on it.

Her stomach gurgled painfully, and she fought against another wave of nausea, biting down on her lip to stop herself from moving. Her mouth filled with saliva, and a small amount escaped her lips to form a pool in the corner of her mouth. The bird jumped forward and tilted its head again. Soon it would be in her blind spot, but also closer. She could either wait for it to be close enough to grab, but risk not being able to see where it was, or attempt to capture the bird while it was in her sight.

'I can reach,' she said with her breath. 'I can reach. I can reach.'

She would need to be quick.

No hesitation.

She licked her lips and shifted her weight on her legs. Her hands twitched, and her heartbeat pulsated uncomfortably in her chest. She counted to three, stared at the bird and shot out an arm.

At the first sign of movement the bird flew backward and Penny caught nothing but air. There it remained as Penny darted forward, hands grasping wildly, until she was centimetres away.

It flew backward again.

'Damn it,' Penny yelled, lurching towards the bird and stumbling over an exposed root. The bird chirped, flapping away in fright as Penny collided into the tree, and settled itself on a branch high above her. It poked its head around a leaf, eyeing Penny with suspicion.

Penny growled at the creature, picking up a rock and throwing it as hard as she could. The stone bounced off the thin trunk of a young tree, several metres away from the bird, and then clattered to the ground.

The bird chirped at her again, a laugh to Penny's ears, and then flew into the canopy. Penny watched her meal escape out of the trees and into the sunset, only looking away when the light forced her eyes to close.

By the time Penny had found anything resembling food the sky had darkened into a thick, ashy violet almost the colour of the bruise beginning to spread across her thigh. She had stumbled through the forest for what must have been hours but she was still unable to find her way back to the river. Her father had made it sound easy. Other animals would need to drink, he had told her. All she had to do was follow their trails back to the water. She had searched fruitlessly for unnaturally snapped branches, or pathways made through the tall grass, but had found nothing, no matter how much she glared.

The soft whispering of trees became a roar whenever she stopped to listen out for running water. She wandered without knowing where to go or whether she was heading backward, or even in one giant circle. Any direction was as safe as any other, after all. She stopped now and then to listen for suspicious noises or to clutch at her stomach as it growled.

Sometimes she would glance uneasily through the trees at the growing darkness in the sky.

Then she would walk faster.

Just when she had decided to give up on food and instead find some sort of shelter for the night, something gently scratched her arm. Penny turned, only just able to catch herself before swaying into a large bramble bush.

A bramble bush dotted with dark purple berries.

Penny looked around, then bit her lip and plucked a berry from the bush. She nibbled at the fruit and waited, longer than she would have liked. It tasted like any other berry, but she couldn't be too careful. When she did not immediately throw up she popped the whole fruit into her mouth, biting down on the soft, sweet skin until it burst. Her mouth filled with juice and saliva. She swallowed it, already reaching out for more. She grabbed handfuls of the berries, replacing each mouthful with another, barely stopping for breath. At one point she thought she was going to vomit, but she swallowed furiously, refusing to let any of the goodness escape her body.

As the bile slipped back down her throat she shuddered and looked up at the bush.

She had eaten every berry she could see, even the ones growing so deeply in the bush that she had scratched her arms pretty badly in several places. Hunger still gnawed at her stomach, but it was duller and easier to manage.

She sighed.

The light had faded to the point that it was becoming difficult to see. There would be no more time to search for anything else, not if she wanted to survive the night. With much hesitation, Penny pulled herself away from the bush. From there it didn't take her long to find a large, hollow tree, thick and grey in comparison to its younger siblings. The tree had a large hole in its trunk, more than big enough for her to squeeze herself inside. She crawled into the tree, tucking her head against her knees and wrapping her arms around her.

It was uncomfortable and cold, but it was safe.

The darkening forest spawned shadows that edged into her line of sight. She watched them creep closer, watched them flicker as if alive. She tried to look away but they were everywhere, and as exhausted as she was, Penny couldn't force her eyes to close. Any time she did she would hear the awful shuffling sound, or the slow scratching of a fingernail in bark.

Pounding on a door.

A few times, despite her better judgement, she found herself drifting into sleep, and waking with a start at the sound of an awful wailing. Each time this happened she pulled herself deeper into the tree, hoping to hide herself within. She stared into the darkness, eyes wild, half-conscious, scanning the forest for any sign of the monsters she knew lurked within.

Eventually no amount of wailing or paranoia could hold sleep at bay, and she fell fully into unconsciousness.

She dreamed of her son.

He was behind a locked door, a door that wouldn't open no matter how much she screamed and slammed her fists against it.

No matter how much her hands bled.

Chapter Three

Penny woke with an itch. A tickle on the side of her foot.

She groaned.

Cold morning air blew through large gaps in the tree trunk, holes she had not seen in the semi-darkness. She shuddered, eyes closed against the encroaching sunlight as her foot itched again. She scratched it against the rough bark of the trunk.

The tickling stopped for half a second, and then resumed.

Penny scratched again, impatient to fall back to sleep before she could remember the full implications of where she was.

The scratching did nothing.

Sighing, she eased her eyes open. The dim, grey light forced its way into her vision. It was too much, too soon, and she winced, blinking furiously as she attempted to become used to the light.

She leaned forward to remove whatever was brushing up against her foot, and watched as a thick, black spider lifted a leg onto her skin.

Penny stared as the creature moved.

It placed another leg on her foot, its silken hair brushing against her.

It began crawling up her leg.

She screamed.

Her leg kicked out and the spider crawled faster in fright, scurrying towards her thigh. Penny screamed again, this time attempting to jump up. Her head slammed into the trunk and she was knocked backward, stunned and confused.

She was trapped.

For a moment she couldn't remember where she was, and flailed her arms and legs around in a desperate attempt to escape. It was another cool gust of air that reminded her of her location. She turned towards it and tumbled out of the trunk on all fours.

She jumped up to her feet, her hands brushing everywhere she could reach. Penny could still feel the itching, could feel the spider crawling beneath her shirt, but no matter how much she looked, she couldn't see it. It was gone.

She rubbed through her hair for good measure, thankful she always kept it as short as she did, and then lifted her leg to make sure the little monster was nowhere near her foot. The moment her weight shifted to her *other* foot, she remembered her injury.

Unfortunately, she remembered too late.

Her foot throbbed in protest as she pressed it into the ground, and though Penny swapped feet immediately to ease the pressure, the dull pain continued to shoot up her leg for quite a while afterwards.

She waited for the pain to fade as much as possible and then placed her foot back down. Gingerly, she tried a few steps forward. Her foot throbbed with each one, but it was a manageable pain and no worse than yesterday. That had to be a good sign.

Still, it wouldn't hurt to clean it up a bit. She had probably smeared it entirely with dirt the evening before. What she needed was a bath.

Penny looked down at her damp, torn vest.

She would also need some new clothes.

It would be much easier to find the river if there weren't so many damn trees, she thought. To Penny, the most logical solution to this problem was to find somewhere without trees. This would be difficult, but not impossible. Though she was surrounded by them, swallowed by them on the ground, there was a place free from branches and leaves.

Up.

She found herself a tree with limbs low enough to provide a decent starting point for climbing, checking it over several times to avoid damaging any other vital body parts, and then she swung onto the first branch.

Then the next.

As she neared the top, the doubts in her mind began to bubble to the surface.

There was no real way she could ever climb high enough to view anything above the canopy. The tree she was climbing probably didn't even go that high. The trunk was already becoming thin enough to sway under her weight. She was afraid that if she climbed any further, the tree would snap.

Penny swallowed back tears of frustration, and climbed back

down, slowly and without the push of hope that had fuelled her ascent.

She landed with a rustle on the mulch-covered ground. She stretched. Sighed. The sound echoed for longer than it should have. Reverberations in a windless world.

A silent world.

Penny stepped backward until her shoulders were pressed against the tree.

The birds had stopped chirping.

She knew what that meant.

How long had she been moving while the world grew still? How long had she been exposed?

Penny held her breath to stop the sound of her chest rising and falling with increased panic. She clamped her eyelids shut with such force that the muscles around her eyes began to ache. Behind her something moved, brushing itself against a tree that rustled like a whisper.

One sentence etched itself into Penny's mind. It repeated itself over and over, gaining in volume and desperation. A crescendo of a single thought.

I don't want to die here.

Footsteps crept closer, slow and clumsy. Each movement was accompanied by a wheezing breath-like sound, a rattling that made her heart shiver.

There was a change in the pressure of the air behind her.

Don't move, it can't see you.

Her mouth dried up.

There were many things she had wanted to do. A thousand ways her life could have been different if it hadn't been for Mary.

Don't breathe. Don't breathe. Don't let it hear you.

She might have grown up surrounded by love and a warm, guiding hand.

She might have been able to stay in a room with the door closed without the risk of nightmares and rising panic.

The daylight will blind it. The daylight will blind it.

Her son might have had a true father figure in his life.

She would have seen him grow up.

It was all *her* fault.

A snap of a branch, close to her ear. A metallic tang in the air. On her tongue.

No, this was not how this was going to go. Mary would not get away with this.

She had already taken someone close to Penny. Penny would not allow it to happen again.

Every muscle in her body tensed.

Her brow furrowed.

Leaves brushed against her face.

Penny wanted to kill Mary, more than anything she had ever wanted before in her life.

The footsteps stopped, but the absence of them was louder still. In the unnatural quiet, Penny heard another sigh, thick and gargled as though made by a throat filled with blood.

Something cold tapped her shoulder and she flinched, digging her fingernails into her thigh. The pain held back the scream, but only just.

Another touch of ice, this time on her nose.

It was beginning to rain.

A sound, like the hissing of a steaming kettle, became a chorus around her as the rain grew heavier. Without thinking, she opened her dry mouth. The rain gushed inside, soothing the cracks and craters she imagined on her tongue. It ran over her closed eyelids and across her hair, laying it flat against her forehead.

She opened her eyes, but could see nothing but the thick torrent of water.

The forest was suddenly alive with noise.

The creature could have moved anywhere. Could be anywhere, and Penny wouldn't have been able to hear a thing. Was it watching her, even now? Had it gone? Could she risk moving? Risk being seen?

Thunder roared overhead.

The creatures were almost fully blind in the daylight, capable of seeing only shadows and murky figures. If Penny moved now, the rain should mask both her body and the sound of her movement. But hadn't her father always told her to remain still when they were near? That any movement might catch their eye, even the slightest glint of her hair in the light? When had he ever been wrong?

Pounding at a door.

Just the rain. Just the rain.

Wait for it to go, or run before it finds her?

Stay or run.

That same question again, but this time Penny had fewer doubts. The rain would cover the sound of her escape, she knew it, but if she was going to move at all she needed to go now. Before the rain stopped and the light vanished and there was nothing left to distract it.

Because once the light was gone, there would be no stopping it.

It would see her. It would catch her. And it would *never* let her go.

A creak behind her.

Wind or monster, it didn't matter.

It was time to leave.

Penny pushed off against the tree and hurled herself through the downpour. Each step was a sickening throb that pulsed from her foot and up her leg. She did not look up from the ground.

She did not look behind her.

Penny ran.

And ran.

She stumbled over groping plants.

Winced as branches clawed at her face. Her neck.

Like small, childlike hands.

She pushed through the burning, through the sweat and the rain, through the screaming of her injuries and her aching limbs. She misjudged the size of a large, sharp rock, and attempted to leap over it. She made it, just, but clipped her foot at the last moment. She twisted in the air and landed in a heap on the floor. The world span so fast her eyes could no longer follow the movement, and she closed them to shut out the nightmare.

It didn't help.

Penny pounded at the wet ground with a fist, trying and failing to push back the dizziness with pure will. She knew she needed food and water, her stomach cramped and gurgled constantly to remind her, but it wouldn't matter how hungry or dizzy she was if one of those things caught up to her now.

Penny pictured thin arms wrapping around her chest with a strength that crushed bones.

She stumbled to her feet, only to fall again, this time crashing into a tree on her way to the muddy floor.

Her stomach clenched, and she doubled over, breathing heavily. Her head was pounding, and blood rushed in her ears. Penny shook her head, attempting to dispel the noise, but the roaring remained.

Penny opened her eyes and looked up.

In front of her, through the trees and the rain, was solid white light.

A clearing.

The river.

Penny staggered out of the clawing grasp of the trees, gasping as the open air and needle-like raindrops battered her bare skin. The wind was bitter, unusual for a day so close to the autumn harvest. Goosebumps prickled against her skin, and she wrapped her arms around her chest, trying to hold in the warmth as she stared out towards the river.

Luckily, it didn't seem like she had travelled too far from her original position. She was at the bottom of a small waterfall, the source of all the roaring and as she had previously suspected, the source of the noise that had caused all the commotion yesterday. Her eyes followed the churning river through the mist.

At the bottom of the waterfall was a mass of sharp-looking rocks and broken wood. Some of the wood was more intact than others, and in places Penny could see the remains of crude boats.

Boats made from bookcases and cabinets.

In her mind, she watched a thin man float away from her on a river much gentler than this one, judged and exiled by his community.

A small crowd of people around her, arms linked.

A glowering woman beside her.

Penny blinked away the visions.

None of that was important.

Keep moving.

The boats were a gift, although an ominous one. There had been people here, possibly people she had known, had spent her life with. People who had not made it to shore, like she had. Penny tried not to picture her own body, lying broken beneath a bookcase at the base of the waterfall. She tried not to think about warm memories of kind faces and wide smiles. Instead, she thought about what else 'people' meant.

Many had been exiled to the river over the years and, now and then, these people took things with them. They were keepsakes and trinkets mainly, items the other house-dwellers would find missing in the days after the departure, but keepsakes can be useful, in the right circumstances.

Penny dreamed of finding old, rusty knives or shards of glass from shattered framed photographs as she edged her way down to the river shore, feet slipping dangerously over slick, wet stone. She managed to get halfway down the slope before a rock wobbled and dislodged beneath her feet.

She lurched forward. As she did, her makeshift bandage tore away from her foot, leaving her wound open to the rocks. Penny screamed and, without thinking, attempted to lift her foot away from the ground. She fell back and slammed into the dirt, shoulders first.

She tumbled downhill, in agony, until she came to a stop at the river's edge, weeping and bleeding.

Penny brushed away her tears with a muddy hand and moved herself to a sitting position. She sniffed, wiped her nose on her vest, and then shuffled over to the water on her knees, dragging her legs behind her.

The river was rippled and rough from the waterfall, but now and then Penny caught a glimpse of herself in the distortion. She had always enjoyed her reflection before, had enjoyed catching glimpses of her face in cutlery or polished glass. She had been pretty, but she could not call herself pretty now. Her face was streaked with sweat and dirt. A trickle of dried blood left a trail down her neck, pooling in her collarbone. Her hair was flat, dirty and the colour of mud. She couldn't bear to look at herself anymore. She winced, cupping water in her hands and let it fall onto her head.

She wiped away the dirt with clean, cold water, rubbing her hair until the chunks of mud fell away in her hands. She washed her body, flinching as the water touched her skin and left her numb. When there was no part of her left to clean, Penny reluctantly lowered her throbbing foot into the river. She hissed as her skin made contact with the surface but pushed on until her foot was completely submerged. With a touch as light as a feather she stroked the bottom of her foot, wiping away dirt and dried blood until the sting of the water became too much and she was forced to pull her foot out of the river. It tingled as the warm air hit.

Penny stretched out an arm behind her, and tugged her ragged shirt away from the rock it had fallen onto. She dunked it into the water, cleaning away as much blood as she could, and then re-tied it around the wound. She drank until her stomach gurgled angrily in protest, and then she drank some more.

She stood.

Swayed.

A small pile of splintered wood was close by, the first of the boats, and Penny limped over to it. She stared down, attempting to peer through the shadows but could see nothing of interest. She bent down and pulled out a loose plank from the pile, freeing it, and then poked at the rest of the wood. It collapsed upon itself with a squelch and a splatter. The wood had been there for quite some time, she guessed. The forest had even started to claim it back. Several of the planks had a dusting of furry green moss, and one had sprouted weeds.

Weeds were of no use to her, and there was nothing else Penny could see.

She gave the pile one last poke before moving on, taking her plank of wood with her and leaning on it like a crutch.

The next wooden mass was more intact, and was still recognis-able as a capsized old wardrobe, roughly moulded into the shape of the boat. It had washed up further towards the forest edge, and she was hoping that would mean it would be drier and less touched by the elements. If nothing else, Penny might be able to use it to make a small shelter. She edged closer and bent her knees to look inside, squinting to make sense of the shadows. There was a putrid smell coming from within that made her eyes water, and Penny scanned the darkness for the source of it. Her eyes fell upon a dark lumpy mass and her heart fluttered.

Penny pulled her head away from the boat and into the fresh air, gasping. She had only seen the shape briefly, too quickly to catch sight of anything recognisable. Still, her mind flashed with images of people she had known. She swallowed, shuddered, and forced herself to calm. She took a breath and then, using her plank, pushed at the boat until it rolled over, revealing the dark shape beneath in a cloud of flies.

Penny flinched and staggered back, fighting the bile that shot up her throat as insects struck her face and chest.

In the dirt, surrounded by broken wood and moss, were the remains of a man. There was not much left of him now. His face had collapsed in on itself, like mould on a slice of bread, and Penny forced herself to turn away before she could look too closely. She didn't want to recognise the man. Didn't want to see a familiar curve of the jaw, or a bulbous nose. Without looking, the man was no one.

And yet, the names of men she had once known filled her thoughts. The man before her could have been any one of them.

Had she known him?

Had she sat across the table from him as they ate breakfast? Or stood at the river's edge as he floated into the distance?

Or had she known him better than that?

Had he told her that he loved her?

Had he held her in the darkness?

Penny bent her knees and heaved into the dirt.

It was some time before she built up the courage to face the corpse once more, and even then she did everything she could to avoid looking at its face. Penny winced and retched as she searched through the shadows for anything of use, her eyes darting everywhere, never lingering. Anything to occupy her mind. Anything to avoid becoming overwhelmed with thoughts of 'I love you', and of a lingering stare drifting away on a boat quite like this one.

Her heart leapt when she saw that, beneath a thick coating of mud, the corpse was wearing a sturdy-looking jacket. Something like that had to be of decent quality to last as long as it had out in the open air.

Penny steeled herself and bent down to grab it.

Something behind her crashed loudly.

She whirled around, plank raised, but could see nothing. No movement or lurking figures. The eerie silence that accompanied the creatures had not settled over the river either.

Perhaps it had been a branch snapping in the wind, she thought, but that didn't sit right with her. Her skin prickled on the back of her neck and she could feel eyes on her.

Watching.

She spat at the ground, still tasting the vomit on her tongue, and then turned back to the old boat. Slowly, taking deep breaths whenever she could, Penny started to pull the jacket off the corpse. It was a type of plastic material, sturdy enough, and seemed to be in better condition than most of the clothes she owned. Penny peeled it away from the rotting skin and immediately turned her back on the corpse. The jacket smelled awful, but looked warm and even semi-waterproof.

Penny dunked it into the river, scrubbing at the plastic with her palms until they grew pink and raw, and then put it on. She pulled the hood over her head and watched as water droplets fell and dripped onto her nose. The jacket was large, far too large for a woman of her size, and lay like ice against her skin. She shivered against the material, but knew that once it dried it would be more than worth it. She could even put up with the smell.

She smiled.

Another noise, rocks tumbling from somewhere she couldn't pinpoint. Too clumsy to be a creature. It had to be an animal.

Penny snarled and swung the plank of wood, holding it in the air like a bat. Her arms were shaking, but not with fear.

'Come on then,' she growled, her voice cracking as she waved her weapon. 'Come on. Come get me!'

The forest did not reply, nor did anything in it. Penny kept the wood aloft for a few more moments, and then lowered it. It might only have been an animal, but it would be safer to leave for now and return to the boats in the morning light.

To her right was the waterfall, and her way home. But she was weak and hungry, and to get past the fall she would have to climb the steep rocks that ran alongside it. The other direction, however, was flat and even ground. Penny thought she could see a mound of rocks close by where she might be able to make a shelter. Maybe if she could rest well tonight, find something to eat, she would be able to climb the rocks tomorrow.

Penny stared at the waterfall, and at the rocks alongside it. She bit her lip, sighed, and reluctantly moved away.

The mound of rocks, it turned out, was a small stone building set into the riverbank. It was too small to be a house, but it seemed to be man-made, with a large wooden door inset with glass. Penny stared at it in suspicion.

Staying in a man-made building would always be risky out here, especially when the river was just outside. Was the benefit of a roof worth the risk of staying in such a dangerous location?

The weather decided for her in the end. After a few rumbles of thunder, the sky cracked and the rain, which had already been a steady downpour, became a torrential storm. The clouds emptied themselves onto the ground below. Penny, unable to see anything but water, ran for the small building. She swung at the door with her plank of wood and it collapsed inwards, crumbling into a pile of damp splinters. Penny peered inside, wrinkling her nose at the dust and cobwebs she could see. It stank of damp and must. Of wood and the dark.

The sky bellowed again, and she forced herself inside.

Penny watched the rain falling and licked her cracked lips.

She shuffled over to the open entrance of the building and cupped her hands until they filled with water. Most slipped through her palms before it could reach her mouth, and she had to repeat this several times to get any relief at all.

She would do anything for a warm, baked potato, or a thin, salty slice of ham. She tried not thinking about food, but that only reminded her not to think about food. Which made her think about food.

The thoughts made her dizzy.

It was too wet to go out and search for something edible now, and with the night approaching, she wasn't sure she'd be able to look for long anyway. Her stomach cramped and gurgled, her head swam as if she was underwater again. She could feel her foot beginning to ache.

If I see another spider, she thought, *I'll eat it.*

She laughed, shoulders shaking, but moving made the world spin and dots appear in her vision.

The colour of the world began to fade.

She slouched down onto the floor, and pulled her knees up to her chest.

She stared at the entrance.

'Did I leave the door open?' she mumbled.

She couldn't see. Everything was foggy and distant.

Grey.

Black.

Nothing.

Before #2

'Mama!' said the boy, darting through the open doors that led into the dining room. He ran over to Penny, clutching something in his hands and showing off the gaps in his tiny rows of teeth.

'Mama, look.'

Penny sighed in her chair and put down the tattered clothing she was attempting, and failing, to fix. The boy waddled over to her feet, and looked up at her, dimples appearing in his soft pink cheeks.

He looked nothing like her when he smiled.

She hated that.

The boy opened his hands a little, and Penny bent over to peer inside. Something on the boy's palm scuttled in the shadows and Penny shot backward, wrinkling her nose.

'What on earth is that?'

'It's a bug! It's shiny.'

'You can't bring that in here. Put it back and wash your hands.'

'It's pretty. Look, Mama. It's pretty!'

'Take it back outside.'

Her voice was stern and the boy looked up, eyes wide.

'I don't want to.'

He stepped backward, but not quickly enough. Penny reached out and grabbed the boy's hands, pulling them open. A large insect flew out, circled the room and shot through the doors. The boy cried out as he watched it fly away. Penny wiped her hands on her shirt.

'That was mine,' said the boy, his lips wobbling as he looked at her.

'No, it wasn't. It's a bug, and you can't own a bug. It needs to fly away and go home.'

The boy's eyes filled with tears. Penny sighed and looked away. She didn't want to see him cry.

'Look,' she said. 'What if the bug has a family? Or a wife? You don't want his wife to be sad, do you?'

'No, you wouldn't want that,' said a quiet voice behind them.

Penny flinched, a small movement she hoped no one else had

seen. She took a slow breath and leaned back into her chair, brushing her hair behind her ear. When she was ready, she looked over her shoulder, smiling.

'Hello, Mary. Can we help you?'

The sullen woman crossed her arms and scowled in the doorway. Light from the window draped across her face, casting shadows that made her look gaunt and tired. Penny watched Mary clench her fists and then step into the room towards her and her son. She walked straight past Penny and over to the boy, sinking to her knees in front of him.

'Hello. That was a very pretty bug you just had. Do you like bugs?'

The boy nodded and smiled, staring bashfully at the floor. He pulled at his t-shirt with little fists.

'Yes. They're fun and they fly. I think they're pretty.'

Mary smiled and pointed to her chest.

'Me too.'

Penny stood, placing herself in front of her son. No longer smiling.

'I was speaking to you, Mary.'

Mary craned her neck up and glowered at Penny, her face ugly with rage. Then she turned back to the boy. Her features softened. She was almost pretty.

'Hey, do you want to come outside with me and look for some more?'

The boy grinned and nodded, his soft hair flapping against his forehead. Penny turned to him, and placed her hands on his shoulders.

'I want you to go to our room.'

'Why? I want to go play. Please, Mama. Please.'

'Go to our room now.'

The boy flinched. His lips trembled and he stared at her, eyes wet and nose running. When it became obvious Penny was not going to change her mind, he ran out of the room.

Mary rose to her feet. Face stern.

'That was rude,' she said. Her voice was calm and featureless, and Penny glared at her.

'What the hell do you think you're doing?'

'You upset him. He wanted to show you the bug and you made him get rid of it.'

'You can't just invite my son to go places with you. Do you not realise how inappropriate that is?'

'I just wanted to play with him. You made him sad.'

'That has absolutely nothing to do with you.'

Mary blinked her glassy eyes, staring through Penny as if she were a phantom.

'Did you know, if you were gone I would be the one to take care of him?'

'What?'

'I'd be the closest thing he had to family. I would take good care of him. I wouldn't make him sad, or frightened.'

Penny scowled. The hairs on her neck stood on end.

Mary continued to stare.

'You're crazy,' Penny said, backing away. 'You're a fucking nut-case.'

'You can think that, if it makes you feel better.'

Mary smiled, showing her teeth. They were yellow and stained. Ugly, like the rest of her.

'Do you know what we'd do?' she continued. 'I'd take him outside and we would go bug catching. We'd spend all day together, writing down all the different bugs we saw. I would get a glass jar and put holes in the lid. Then we'd pick our favourite and keep it inside. It would be a pet for him, and he could watch it all the time. He'd like that. Have you ever done anything like that for him?'

Penny took a larger step back, trying to reach the door. She kept her head held high. She couldn't let Mary know she was frightened. There was no telling what she would do.

'I honestly could not care less about what you would do. He's not your son, is he? He's mine. And we won't be putting any bugs in jars.'

'Why, don't you want to do something he likes? Don't you want to make him happy?'

'We do plenty of things he likes, and he is happy. This is none of your business.'

'It might be, one day.'

Mary smiled at her again.

Penny remembered that smile in the dark, mocking her.

I can't open the door, said a voice in her head. Mary's voice. Penny's heartbeat quickened. Her palms were greasy with sweat.

The light from outside that had been streaming in from the doors faded, like a candle blown out in a dim room. The sun-bleached curtains either side of the doorway rippled in the breeze. Mary spun until she was facing the outside.

'It looks like it's going to rain,' she said, her voice slow and unnatural.

Penny frowned, reaching back for the doorknob behind her. Her fingers grasped cool metal, and she twisted the handle with relief. She turned quietly and pushed the door open. She was almost free. She just needed to leave the room without Mary seeing her.

Penny thought she had made it, and was halfway out of the door, ready to run, when the strange woman called out to her.

'Penny?' she said.

Penny froze, not turning. Not looking.

'What?'

'Do you ever regret what happened? What you did?'

Penny forced herself to turn back into the room.

'No. Do you?'

She waved, smiled and closed the door.

Her heart beat painfully in her throat.

The boy was in bed when she entered the room, the blanket covering his face and his feet sticking out the other side. She bit her lip, considered what she was going to say, and closed the door.

The boy jumped, and then retreated further under his blanket.

'What are you doing?' said Penny, as kindly as she knew how.

'Nothing,' mumbled the boy.

'Are you upset?'

'No.'

'Doesn't sound like it.'

The boy said nothing.

Penny walked over and sat on the bed. It squeaked beneath her weight. The boy pulled away from her.

'You have to be careful with strangers; you know that, don't you?'

'Mary's not a stranger,' said the boy, muffled beneath the blanket, his voice miserable. Penny dug her fingernails into her palm.

'Sometimes people aren't what they seem to be. People that seem nice might not be. Do you understand?'

'No.'

She thought of a hand around hers. A weathered, kind face and eyes that twinkled in the firelight.

'Sometimes a person will want something, and they will tell lies to get what they want. They aren't nice people.'

'Mary's nice.'

'No, she is not. She's only being nice to make me mad. She wants me to be mad at you. Do you want that? Does that sound nice to you?'

Beneath the blanket the boy began to sniff and hiccup. Penny sighed and lowered her head. She reached out to place a hand on his shoulder, and then drew it back.

'I'm sorry,' she whispered. 'I didn't mean it, okay? Mary is a nice person. I just want you to be careful. I was worried. Will you be careful for me?'

The boy said nothing.

Penny stepped away from the bed and moved to the window.

The clouds were a dark angry grey, a flat sheet of slate. Something tapped against the window, and then again. Penny watched as a droplet ran down the length of the glass, leaving a trail behind it.

In the distance, thunder rumbled, a low animal roar in the sky.

Penny stood silent and still, and watched the rain falling against the forest backdrop.

The rain always calmed her. Some combination of the pitter-patter of water drops and the dim sleepy light, she supposed. She wasn't sure.

Perhaps she liked the rain because it seemed to make everyone else miserable.

That seemed more like her.

She placed a finger against a droplet on the glass and followed it down. The droplet reached another bead of water, paused, and then swallowed it. The bigger, stronger, droplet ran towards the bottom of the frame and slipped away.

Chapter Four

It was warm.

Did she have a fever?

She didn't recall ever having a fever before.

Fevers were supposed to be unpleasant, though. Weren't they? They could kill you. This wasn't unpleasant at all. It was nice. Comforting. She could even smell something. Food.

Meat.

Had she had a fever when she was a child? Back when her father was still around? Maybe. She couldn't remember. She missed him. Was he here? Was he going to take care of her?

She hoped so.

Maybe she was back at the house. Were they making her something to eat? That would be nice. It was really warm.

Her mouth filled with saliva, the liquid running out of the corner of her lips and trailing down the side of her face. How could she still have so much saliva? She was thirsty. Penny stretched a little and something hard pushed against her back. She was sitting, propped up against something, her hands resting in her lap. Had she fallen asleep like that? She didn't think so. It was nice and warm, though. Where was she again?

Penny saw a flicker of light behind her eyelids, which was strange because the sun didn't flicker.

Why was it so warm?

Did she have a fever?

Her head started to pound, an awful throbbing that came with every beat of her heart and every breath. She wanted to rub her eyes but her arms were too heavy to lift all the way. Penny tried to stretch them out in front of her instead. Heat tickled the backs of her hands.

That wasn't right.

Penny prised her eyes open, only a little but enough to see dancing shadows and a bright, warm light.

Orange light.

Fire.

Penny shot forward with a gasp.

Fire. There couldn't be fire.

She needed to put it out.

They would see the light.

They would follow it.

They would find her.

She pulled herself towards the flames, still groggy from sleep.

She did not move.

Why wasn't her body listening?

She fought with herself and became aware of a tightness around her shoulders and stomach.

Penny looked down and cried out when she saw the thick rope around her. She struggled against it, pulling with all the strength she had left, and fell back, panting and scanning her location like a cornered animal.

Her prison seemed to be a small cave. From the mouth she could see the tops of trees and in the distance, just about visible, was the river.

She wasn't too far, then. But how had she got here in the first place? Had she been sleeping so deeply someone had simply walked over and dragged her away?

Had she been that vulnerable?

The thought of anyone, anything, being able to get that close without her knowledge made her feel sick.

The cave itself was tiny, with room only for the large fire in its centre and a makeshift bed comprised of various fabrics and leaves. The floor beside the bed was strewn with a selection of roughly carved wooden bowls, several filled with water and herbs. Behind them, several blankets hung from the wall. They swayed to and fro, but never allowed her a glimpse of whatever was behind.

Penny stared at the blankets and frowned. She raised a hand, just as far as the ropes would allow, but felt nothing.

She watched the curtains move.

How were they moving without any breeze?

Dread came over her, cold and wet.

There was someone, something, moving behind the curtains.

Penny strained against the ropes again, holding her breath and shaking with the effort. Her hands pulled against them and she dug her feet into the stone floor as she pushed. Her foot slipped and shot sideways into a small pile of firewood. The logs toppled to the floor, clattering loudly in the cavern.

They would know she was awake now.

Penny pushed and strained, crying out as the ropes dug tightly into her. She closed her eyes and wriggled breathlessly, stopping only when a strong pair of hands pushed her back. She shuddered against their touch.

A dry, cracked voice began cooing to her, brushing her hair from her eyes. Stale, warm breath violated her ears.

'Shh,' said the voice, 'shh now. Don't fight, don't fight. Shh. It's okay. You're okay.'

'Get away,' Penny cried. 'Let me go.'

She tried to push against the being that held her in place but she was far too weak to make any difference. The man held her down, firm and unmoving.

'No, no, no, don't fight. Don't fight. You're hurt. Poor love. My poor darling. Shh, now.'

Rough hands pawed at Penny's face, stroking her cheek. Her eyes snapped open and she pulled her face away from the man's touch, glaring at him.

'Don't touch me,' she spat.

The man pulled his hands away, looking pained.

He had been out here for a while, that much was obvious, and the forest had taken its toll on his face. He was thin but strong looking, and the parts of his haggard face not obscured by mud were hidden by wiry hair and a large, untamed beard. The only features to betray his humanity were the man's sharp, hazel eyes and the deep, dark-purple circles below them. There was something familiar about those eyes, about the man himself, but Penny couldn't focus on the images that fluttered through her mind. It was like she was experiencing the ghost of a dream – anytime she came close to the truth, the image would simply fade away. As she stared, the man smiled at her, revealing a broken graveyard of stained, brown teeth.

Penny wrinkled her nose.

'Why am I here?'

'I saved you,' said the man. 'Found you, saved you. I knew it was you.'

Penny stared at his face.

'I don't know you,' she said, flinching slightly at the uncertainty in her voice. 'Please let me go.'

The man pointed at himself with a dirty finger and smiled wider.

'It's okay, Pen. It's me. We'll be okay now. We're all together. Just like you wanted.'

Penny's heart skipped a beat.

'What did you say?' she said.

'Shh. Shh, now. You need to rest. You're hurt. You can't—'

'What did you call me?'

Her voice was shaking, her eyes wide. A ghostly finger traced the length of her spine and she shivered. The man cocked his head, a deranged impersonation of a bird.

'What's wrong, Pen? Are you in pain? Are you—'

'*What* did you call me?'

The man smiled. It would have been a gentle smile, if his eyes had held any form of sanity.

'You never could let anyone finish a sentence,' he said, and then laughed, a sound more like a hoarse wheeze than anything else. Penny winced at the odour leaking from his mouth, watching as he scratched his beard, staring at her with his stupid grin.

His eyes twinkled.

She knew those eyes. How did she know them?

The wild man paused and then opened his mouth in shock. Penny could see a wet, brown lump at the back of his throat.

'Oh! I forgot. Oh dear. Wait there, Pen, wait there.'

He rose to his feet, knees clicking, and scurried off behind the swaying curtain. Penny watched him go. She tried to take in every part of him, every inch, no matter how disgusting. He knew her. She knew him too, somewhere deep in the recesses of her mind. His eyes, his smile – he even called her 'Pen'. Nobody ever called her that, not anymore. She had only ever let her father call her that. How dare this man use that name?

But then, there had been someone else who called her Pen.

It's not possible.

The man began to murmur behind the curtain and Penny caught the odd phrase here and there.

'Shh, shh, stay still,' he murmured. 'Calm down. It's okay.'

Was he talking to her? Could he see her starting to struggle? She froze, glaring at the curtain as the man began to speak again. Trying to catch a secretive glimpse of his face to quell her ridiculous thoughts.

'No, little one. Don't do that. It's okay. Daddy's here.'

Little one? God, he really was mad.

Imagining children.

Calling himself 'Daddy'.

Another impossible thought flickered into life and she pushed it away. Whether she knew him or not, the man was obviously unstable. Penny needed to leave. Right now.

She bent her arms until they were behind her back, and then fumbled for the knot.

Behind the curtain the man began to hum, a gentle soothing song that set Penny's teeth on edge.

She knew that song, didn't she?

The man moved from humming to singing, his voice soft despite its cracking. A voice filled with tenderness.

'Hush, little baby, don't say a word. Daddy's gonna buy you a mockingbird. And if that mockingbird won't sing, Daddy's gonna buy you a diamond ring.'

Penny was sure her heart had ceased to beat.

Her lungs stopped working.

She couldn't breathe.

Those same hazel eyes on a clean, beardless face.

A gentle man singing to her swollen stomach.

A lingering gaze floating away on a boat like the one she had found beside the river.

'Oh shit,' she whispered.

She wasn't going to die in the forest, not anymore.

It would be him that killed her.

The man finished singing and came out from behind the curtains, stopping to make sure they were fully closed. Only then did he turn to her. Penny's cheeks reddened with shame as their eyes locked, but she kept her head high. Staring him down.

'Lewis,' she said.

It was not a question.

The man grinned, brown teeth almost black in the shadows of the cave.

'You remember me,' he said.

Penny nodded and forced herself to smile. She remembered he had liked her smile. Hopefully he still did.

'Yes. Yes, of course. I'm sorry, Lewis. You look… different. I didn't expect to…'

He scrambled over to her, falling onto his knees and clutching her face in his hands. He smelled sour.

'You remember me. I knew you would. I always hoped for this. Not like this, not you weak and tired, but for you to be here. With us. I knew this would happen. I just knew it. You don't know how happy I am, Pen. I'm glad I found you.'

'How did you find me, Lewis?'

He let go of her and pointed out of the cavern mouth, towards the river.

'I can see most things from here. Most important things. I watch for people coming down the river. I take their clothes. Boots. It's all important. Oh! Clothes. You need new clothes. I'll—'

'Just—' Penny started, her voice raised. She stopped. It would be no use shouting. She took a breath, composed herself. 'In a minute, please. You saw me on the river?'

'Yes! Well, no. I saw someone, but you were gone when I got there so I knew the person might be around. Be alive. No one's ever alive. They just lie back and wait. Isn't that sad? I looked everywhere to get to you before you got hurt. I saw you by the waterfall when I was out searching for food and I couldn't believe it! I was sure it was you, but I had to check. When I saw you sleeping in the little house

I couldn't help myself. I tried to wake you, talk to you, but you were sleepy, delirious, poor thing. You didn't even wake when I touched you! I was worried, but I managed to carry you back here. Back to us. I'm stronger than I look.'

And then you tied me up, she thought.

'How are you alive, Lewis? If no one ever makes it, how did you?'

He cocked his head.

'The woman found me. Helped me. Gave her to me.'

The forest was becoming rather too crowded for Penny's liking.

'Who are you talking about?'

Lewis didn't answer, he only smiled.

Penny flushed red again.

'Look,' she said. 'Lewis, I don't know what they told you... before it happened. But it wasn't me. I had nothing to do with it. You know I would never say anything like that, not about you.'

Penny smiled, and managed to stretch out her arm, placing her hand on his without wincing too noticeably. He looked down at it, eyes glazed.

Penny continued, this time in a whisper.

'It was Mary, you know that, don't you? She was jealous of us. Jealous of what we had. Our child. Our family. She said all those things.' She leaned closer still. 'She separated us.'

Lewis snatched his hand away, staring into space.

'I need to make you some food,' he said, all expression gone from his voice.

He rose to his feet, his eyes blank, and removed himself from the cave. Penny watched him leave and bit her lip.

He was gone for what must have been hours, leaving Penny alone with her thoughts and with whatever was behind the curtain, if there was anything at all. She had given up struggling against the rope very quickly and instead found herself unwillingly drifting between sleep and consciousness.

Lewis returned at sunset with two skinned rabbits, which he skewered and placed over the fire. He picked up a bowl of water, moved back over to Penny and held the water to her lips.

'Drink,' he said.

Penny sat up and tried to reach to take the bowl for herself but Lewis snatched it away, a look of horror on his face. He waited for Penny to put her arms down and held out the bowl again. She sighed and allowed him to trickle water into her mouth. She took an initial sip out of politeness and then swallowed down larger mouthfuls with greed. She was thirstier than she had thought. This satisfied Lewis and he took away the bowl.

'Lewis,' she croaked, holding back a coughing fit as the water slipped down her throat. 'How have you managed to survive this long? You even have a fire. Why haven't they found you?'

He cocked his head again. Childlike.

'Who?'

Penny frowned.

'What do you mean "who"? You know who. Don't you remember blocking out the light before the night came? Moving only in the day? We've spent our whole lives hiding in a giant house on a hill just to stay alive. What the hell is wrong with you?'

The words left her mouth before she could think and she began to stutter an apology. Lewis seemed not to have noticed. He was staring at her, his brow furrowed as if trying to piece together her words.

'I don't understand. There isn't anyone. Just me and the woman and her... Oh! Oh, I know. The little ones. Oh, they're no bother.'

Penny almost laughed.

'Little ones? Are you mad? They're monsters, not... children. Don't you remember what they can do? What they *will* do if they see the fire? See you?'

He waved her away.

'It's fine, it's fine,' he said. 'We're way too high for them to see us and they aren't all bad. The woman helps me. She's good with them. Knows them. I'll take you to her soon. When you're better. She can help.'

'Lewis, I don't understand.'

Again, he ignored her. Instead, he leaned over, his expression serious, and placed both hands on her knees.

'How... how is Mary? Is she well?'

The turn in the conversation frustrated her, but Penny was in no position to argue. She sighed slowly to allow herself some time to think.

'After everything she's done to me, to us,' she said, eventually, 'you still care?'

'She's… she's my wife. Was my wife. I loved her.'

'You said you loved me.'

'I did. Do. I do.'

'She put me here. Knocked me out, put me in a boat and shipped me off without anyone else knowing. She was always jealous of me. Of us. Now she has our son and there's nobody around to stop her.'

'We did wrong by her. I never meant to. I didn't want to hurt her. She was always a gentle woman. She wouldn't have done this. She wouldn't have hurt you.'

'She's a snake,' Penny snarled, a tear rolling down her cheek and onto her lips. 'She deserved everything that happened to her. She was always cruel to you. I told you she was. I was never cruel to you, was I?'

'No. No, you weren't.'

'I always loved you, Lewis. She didn't. She only wanted to be a mother. She was using you. But she was just like everyone else in the end. Not like us. We were special, Lewis. I don't care what they say the reason for the infertility is. *That's* why we were able to have a baby. Don't you see that?' She paused. Looked down. 'You aren't going to leave me again, are you?'

Her voice cracked.

Another tear fell.

Lewis grabbed her and pulled her into a tight hug. He stroked her hair roughly, kissing it, and Penny had to stop herself from flinching at his touch.

'No. I won't leave you,' he said. 'Never. Never again.'

'Do you forgive me? I should have defended you, stopped them from sending you away, but she frightened me. I'm sorry. Please forgive me. Please.'

'Yes. We forgive you. We forgive you, Penny. My darling.'

Penny sniffed. Stared at the wall.

'Lewis?'

'Yes, Pen? Yes, darling?'

'Why do you keep saying "we"? Is the woman you mentioned here?'

He pushed her back until they were nose to nose. His breath made her eyes water, but she forced a sweet smile.

'No, she's not here. Far away. But she gave me a gift. A daughter. Our daughter.'

Penny shivered.

'Your... daughter?'

Lewis smiled at her.

Penny knew what he was going to say, even before he spoke the words aloud.

'Oh yes. A pretty little girl. One of the little ones from the forest.'

Chapter Five

The air around her fell still, like ice on a frozen lake.

She couldn't breathe or move.

He didn't mean one of those monsters was here. It wasn't possible. They were untameable. They sought and found and ran, and grabbed and squeezed and squeezed until the breath was gone and there was nothing of you left.

Her knuckles turned white. She began struggling against the rope.

She needed to get away.

Needed to run from the creature behind the curtain.

The ropes rubbed and burned against her bare skin.

She had been here for too long already.

It was only a matter of time.

Penny looked up at Lewis, pleading with her eyes, unable to work her mouth, but he just looked at her with his head cocked. Confused.

'What's wrong?' he asked. 'Aren't you pleased?'

'Quiet,' she hissed in reply. 'We need to go. Let me loose. I need to go. Please.'

'I don't understand.'

'Under—? One of those things— It's here. Oh God. We need to go. We aren't safe!'

'I know she's here. I brought her here. She was a gift.'

'Are you crazy?'

'I don't understand, Pen. Why are you whispering? Are you angry?'

'Be quiet! It will hear you. Please let me go. Please.'

'She.'

'What?'

'She, not it. She's a she. A girl. A pretty little girl.'

'Oh God. Please, please let me go.'

'Besides, she can't hear you. Can't hear anything. She's deaf.'

Penny stopped struggling.

'What?'

'Deaf. And blind. Almost. The woman fixed her for me. I thought I told you that?'

He stroked her cheek as if in a daze and she pulled away, eyes wide.

'Lewis, that's not possible. It will kill you. It will kill both of us. We need to go.'

'She's been living with me for months. She wouldn't hurt a fly. She's not like the others, Pen. She loves me.'

'Months?' she stammered. 'That's not possible. How has it been here so long? How are you still *alive*?'

'I told you, she won't hurt us. Even if she wanted to, and she doesn't Pen I promise, she can't. She can't see me, you or anything. She doesn't even know we're here.'

'You're lying. It has to know you're here. It will see the fire. It will see us.'

'She can't. I promise. See, her eyes our different to ours. Usually they can only see well in the dark. They're nocturnal, I think. The day is too bright for them, too distracting. It stops them dead. But they love the light. They search for it at night, like moths. The woman says it reminds them of us. That they head towards it to find us. Isn't that sad?'

'No,' Penny spat.

Lewis frowned.

'You're wrong. They miss us. They want to find us. That's sad.'

'Lewis, why doesn't it know you're here? Why hasn't it killed you?'

'Because she's not like the others, Pen. She's special. The woman changed her. She can't see anything at all in the dark. As long as she's behind the curtain, she's blind. The curtain blocks the fire and it keeps her calm and happy and safe, and I blindfold her on extra bright days.'

'And what happens if the curtain falls? Or the blindfold slips? What happens if the light gets through?'

Lewis smiled.

'It won't.'

'Lewis, you have to listen to me. That thing is a monster. They have killed *millions* of us.'

'She's harmless.'

'No it is not. You keep it tucked away in the shadows because the moment it sees the light it will *kill* you and you know that. It's why you have that fucking curtain in the first place. They are demons. Devils.'

For a flicker of a moment Lewis seemed to snarl. Penny flinched, but when she opened her eyes he had already relaxed back into a smile.

'You're wrong,' he said. 'I'll show you.'

He dived at her, reaching behind her back and began to fumble with the rope before she realised what was happening.

She caught on pretty quickly.

Penny's body grew cold and she could feel a trickle of sweat run down her neck.

'Lewis, whatever you're about to do, please don't.'

'Shh, it's fine. You'll see. You'll love her, just wait.'

'Please, Lewis.'

He did not seem to hear her, his attention never swaying from the rope. As soon as the pressure around her body eased, Penny lurched away, but Lewis was faster. He grabbed her wrist and began to pull her to her feet, then across the room.

Towards the thick, tattered curtain.

She dug her heels into the rock but the forgotten pain in her foot flared up, white hot. Lewis didn't acknowledge her cry of pain and she had to limp after him to keep up.

They stopped next to the curtain, close enough to smell its dry musk. Lewis smiled, and then shoved her hand into the darkness beyond the fabric.

She fought, but Lewis had developed a strength he never had back at the house. Her hand went wherever he moved it and Penny could do nothing to stop him. She clenched her hand into a fist, pleading with Lewis under her breath, her words a jumble. He did not look at her. He just smiled, gently, at the curtain.

'You'll see,' he said again, and tugged her arm deeper into the cavern.

Something soft brushed against her knuckles, tickling her skin.

Long and silky.

Penny pleaded louder.

Hair.

It was hair.

And it was moving.

Penny shrieked and pulled away. Her wrist, slick with sweat, slipped from Lewis' grasp. She stumbled backward, knocking the curtain as she moved.

The fabric started to sway.

Back and forth.

Soft firelight bounced off the wall behind the curtain.

Something sat in the darkness, staring at the wall.

Its back to them.

She had time to see the glint of blonde hair and grey, leather-like skin before Lewis pushed Penny to the ground. Her head bounced against stone, but she did not cry out. Lewis stared towards the curtain, his face a bloodless white.

They did not move, frozen together in an awkward embrace.

Silent.

A tear ran down Penny's face onto the ground.

The curtain rocked, back and forth.

Back and forth.

From beyond, Penny heard a rustling sound, like fabric pulled across rough stone. The rustle became a sigh. The sigh became a voice.

'Haaaa.'

That noise again. But what did it mean? Was the creature waking up? Standing up? Moving closer and closer and—

The curtain calmed and the noise stopped.

Penny and Lewis did not move. They stared at the curtain, waiting for it to fall completely still. When it finally stopped, Lewis sat up, moving away from her slowly, as if in shock. Penny rolled to her knees and pushed her hair away from her face.

'Lewis,' she started. 'I'm so—'

Lewis smacked her across the face, hard, and she rocked backward.

Her cheek burned.

She raised a hand and pressed it against her cheek, her mouth open. Unable to speak.

Lewis groaned. He pawed at her and pulled her close to him before she could even think to resist. He nuzzled into her hair and Penny could smell his sweat.

'I'm sorry,' he wailed. 'I'm sorry. I'm really sorry. I love you. Don't be mad. I won't do it again. Never. I love you. I love you.'

Penny said nothing.

Lewis began to rock her in his arms. He kissed her hair, stroked it, brushed her skin as she lay limp and devoid of spirit. After a while, he guided her back to her seat on the floor and re-tied her. When he finished and Penny had still not spoken, he lifted her chin until she had no choice but to look into his eyes.

She kept her face blank, cool.

'Do you forgive me?' he asked, eyes watery and red.

Penny pinched the skin on her leg and smiled.

'Of course, Lewis. I love you.'

He wailed again and clung to her once more, his body heaving as he sobbed into her hair. A big, ugly tear ran down her face, catching at the corner of her mouth. She licked it. Swallowed. Her face blank.

As Lewis' tears subsided he began to murmur to himself, curling up and snuggling into her neck.

'We'll be okay,' he said. 'We're together now. We're a family again. We'll be okay. All of us. We'll be happy, Pen. They can't tear us apart again. I love you, Pen.'

'I love you too,' replied Penny, digging her nails into her palm and staring out towards the river.

Towards the forest.

They ate the rabbit in silence, Lewis staring at her with a dreamy smile as a piece of meat clung to his beard and swayed with his breath. She watched it move, her stomach churning, but forced herself to eat every mouthful in front of her, regardless. There was no telling when she would next eat properly, and Penny even licked at the bones that remained, scraping at them with her teeth to get to the leftover meat. Lewis had thankfully allowed her to feed herself, but had made her promise not to move around too much as she did so.

'You're still weak,' he had explained as he placed the small wooden bowl of meat into her lap. 'You mustn't strain yourself.'

Penny, of course, agreed to everything.

She gnawed at a bone and stared at the man in front of her. Her stomach gurgled, warning her not to eat another bite if she didn't want it to all come back up again. Still she eyed the piece of meat hanging from Lewis' mouth. Lewis followed her gaze, removed the meat and popped it into his mouth.

'No, Pen,' he said, chewing with his mouth open. 'You can't eat too much at once. You'll be sick.'

She glared at him in the firelight, pushed back her hair and smiled sweetly.

'Sorry, Lewis. You're right. I don't think I could eat another bite, it was wonderful.'

He smiled in reply, flushing with pride like a child. Chest puffed out.

'You cooked for me before, do you remember?' Penny continued, leaning towards him as far as she could manage. 'I said I was hungry, and you went and stole some things from the kitchen for me. Even when Mary was in control of you, you were still so kind to me. Do you remember that?'

He smiled at the floor and rubbed his ankle, thin and bony.

'I remember,' he said.

'Do you know when I first realised I loved you?'

'No. No, I—'

'I was walking in the hallway of the third floor. I wanted to stretch my legs, but it was raining. Too dark to go outside. I walked near your door and heard Mary shouting at you. Screaming at you. I didn't want to eavesdrop, but I was shocked. I thought that she might hurt you. I went to your door to make sure everything was okay. I was about to go in. I heard her call you pathetic.'

'Yes. She thought she might have been pregnant, she had been excited. Thrilled. But then it turned out she... wasn't. She was very upset.'

'That was no excuse for her language. Those awful things she said. I saw her start to hit you. But do you remember what you did? You hugged her. Even while she tried to hit you. You were always kind to her. I fell in love with you then. She never deserved you.'

'I never understood.'

'Pardon?'

'I never understood why you loved me, I could never understand it. You are beautiful. Mary tried to tell me that you would never love someone like me. She said you were using me because you hated her.'

Penny's mouth twitched.

'I did hate her,' she said. 'I hated her more than anything. Do you know why? Because of what she did to you. What she did to everyone around her.'

'But someone like you... with someone like me.'

Penny's lip trembled and she stared up at Lewis, her eyes brimming with tears.

'Even now, when we're finally together, you don't believe I love you?'

She allowed a tear to fall. Lewis had the decency to look away in shame.

Penny's voice trembled.

'I knew it. You still love her, don't you? You never loved me. Don't you know what she did? We're here because of her!'

'Yes!' he said, and scrambled over on his knees. 'Yes. We're together now. She brought us together.'

'But you love her.'

'No. You. Always you.'

'Do you promise?'

'Yes. Yes, I promise.'

Penny smiled and held his cheek.

They slept against the rock, Penny upright and uncomfortable, Lewis wrapping his arms around her as if desperate to steal her warmth. The rope of her bindings dug into her stomach as she stared into the darkness.

Stared at the curtains.

Imagining small limbs twitching in the dark.

She slept, eventually, and dreamed of a man that wasn't Lewis.

A better man.

Stronger and kinder, with a voice like smoke. A man who protected her from those creatures, instead of leaving her bound before one like a sacrificial lamb.

She woke first in the morning, stiff and achy but much better for the food she had eaten the previous evening. Lewis was curled into a ball at her side, his mouth open as he slept.

Disgusting.

She frowned and looked away.

As her mind grew sharper and the fog of sleep lifted, Penny began to check her body for damage. The wound at the base of her skull seemed to be in much better condition, and though it was sore to touch it was no longer as painful as it had been. Her foot, on the other hand, had not improved at all.

She stretched it slowly, wincing as the skin around the wound tightened and pulled.

'What's wrong?'

Penny jumped.

Lewis was kneeling, staring at her.

When had he moved? She hadn't heard a thing.

'Oh, Lewis,' she said, placing a hand against her chest. 'I didn't think you were awake.'

'What's wrong?'

'It's nothing. I hurt my foot a few days ago. It's a little sore.'

Lewis threw off the coat they had been using as a blanket and picked up her foot, ignoring her protests. He twisted it in the morning light, frowning.

'Why didn't you tell me?'

'It's not anything to worry about, it's just a little cut. It's fine. I just need to rest it.'

'It looks bad. Very bad. It's not clean. You need medicine.'

'It will be fine, don't worry. Why don't we have breakfast? I'm still very hungry.'

'Pen, your foot could get infected. That's bad. I need to clean it.'

'I told you, it's fine.'

'No.'

Lewis began to squeeze, pushing a finger into the wound until Penny gasped. Her vision began to blur. Her hands slammed against the stone floor.

It hurt.

Oh God, it hurt.

'See? It's painful. Let me clean it. Let me help you.'

'Okay. Okay, Lewis. You can clean it. Please. Please stop.'

Lewis released the pressure, smiling at her as if she were a child. Tears ran down her face.

'I knew you'd agree,' he said. 'I'll go get some fresh water. Wait there.'

He dropped her foot and lumbered to his feet, grabbing some empty bowls as he scurried out of the cave. He was gone before Penny, panting and still tied to a rock, could cry out for him not to leave her alone.

Her foot throbbed and she could still feel the pressure of his long, dirty finger pushing into her skin. The last sound of his footsteps faded and the silence became overwhelming. Soon all Penny could think about was the presence of the thing behind her, staring into the darkness. Waiting for the light. She bit her lip, glared at the curtains, and leaned over, stretching out her arms towards the pile of firewood beside her.

Lewis returned far too quickly, with two bowls of water hooked onto one arm and a handful of plants that resembled small onions clutched in his left hand. He sniffed at them, took a bite, and sat down cross-legged in front of her. He pushed some of the plants into her hands, and used a rock to crush some of the others into one of the bowls. Water sloshed around as he worked, and Penny scowled from the man, to the plants in her hand. She wrinkled her nose.

'What's this?'

'Breakfast,' said Lewis, mashing the water.

'But what is it?'

'Onions, I think. Some mint. I'm putting some in the water too. It's good. Eat.'

'Can't we have rabbit again? I'm hungry.'

Lewis dunked his hand in the water and pulled out a clump of thick green paste, which he then smeared onto her foot. Her wound started to sting, but Penny did her best not to flinch. Lewis looked up at her and gestured to the plants in her hand with a nod.

'This is good for you. It will help. Eat it.'

Penny scowled, sighed, and then bit into one of the plants that looked quite like an onion. It was crunchy, and it reminded her a little of garlic, but milder. It was edible, at least.

'Eat the green bit, too,' Lewis said, washing a strip of fabric in the water and then wrapping it around her foot. Penny ate everything, though the stalk was bitter and left a foul aftertaste. Lewis watched while she wiped her mouth, and handed her the bowl of clean water. She drank it all, staring over the edge of the bowl at Lewis as he threw a few branches onto the fire.

'Better?' he asked as he turned back to her.

'Much,' said Penny, her voice flat. If Lewis noticed the sarcasm in her tone, he didn't mention it. Instead he nodded in approval, and walked over to the curtain.

Penny's mouth grew dry, and a flutter of panic burst in her chest at the thought of the thing behind the fabric. She pushed it aside.

There was no time to be afraid.

'Wait,' she said. 'Wait a minute. Please.'

He stopped and looked at her. Penny moved her gaze to the ground.

'I wanted to thank you,' she said. 'For taking care of me, I mean.'

'I'm happy to help you, Pen. You know that.'

'I know. But still, I'd like to thank you properly.'

She shuffled, feeling the firewood in her back pocket pressing against her skin.

'If you untie me, I could hug you properly. I've missed hugging you. You were gone for such a long time.'

'Oh, Pen,' Lewis said. He stepped forward, towards her, and then stopped himself. He narrowed his eyes.

'If I let you go, you won't run away?'

'What?' she said, and then laughed. 'Why would I run?'

'You have to promise. Promise me you won't run away.'

'Of course I won't.'

'Say it.'

'I promise.'

'Swear.'

Penny smiled and crossed her heart. With a strong, clear voice she said, 'I swear on the life of our new daughter'.

That seemed to satisfy Lewis. He nodded and stepped over to her, bending down to fiddle with the rope, which quickly seemed to slink to the floor. The tightness around her chest fell away. Penny's smile widened.

She stood, stretched and wrapped her arms around Lewis, holding him close. Pushing into him. Digging her hands into his matted hair.

'I told you, Lewis. I love you.'

Lewis did nothing, frozen to the spot in shock. He shivered and then, slowly, returned her embrace. He placed his head against her neck, breathing deep. His warmth surrounded her, the scent of his sweat cloying and strong enough to taste.

'I'm really happy, Lewis.'

'Me too, Pen.'

'You know,' she said, twirling his long hair around a finger, 'I was thinking about our daughter. I miss our son, but now I don't have to, do I?'

'Exactly. That's right. We have a new family.'

'Right. A new family.'

She paused, took a deep breath.

'I'd like to meet her. Could I?'

He pushed her back, one hand on each shoulder and stared into her face. Searching for a sign he had misheard, she guessed.

'Really? Do you mean it?'

She poked his nose.

'Of course.'

He threw his arms into the air, shouting so loud Penny jumped despite herself. He clutched at his face, as if he was going to cry, unable to stand still.

'Oh, Pen. I'm so happy. She'll be happy too. I'll get her ready, right now. Just wait. Wait there.'

He flapped around, looking lost, grinned and ran behind the curtain. Penny watched him go, smiling until he vanished completely from sight. Once he was gone, the smile became a grimace.

She didn't have long now. She had to be quick.

Penny pulled the stick of firewood from her back pocket and pushed one end into the campfire. She waited, biting her lip, until the end caught light with a snap, then walked over to the curtain and placed the flame against the corner of the fabric.

The curtain was thick but dry.

It did not take long.

Penny thought about many things she could have said at that moment. Something dramatic or clever.

'Only my father calls me Pen, arsehole' or 'I love you, Lewis'.

In the end, she left without saying a word, stopping only to grab her jacket from the pile by the entrance.

She was halfway out of the cave when she heard him scream.

She turned, eyes lit up with pride and firelight, a smirk dancing on the corner of her lips. Beyond the fire were two figures: one large, one small. A section of curtain, charred and black, fell to the ground in ashes.

Penny saw a sinister black eye.

A small mouth turned upwards in the mockery of a smile.

A monster in a child's form.

The creature shot forward, grinning face blurred by the speed at which it moved. Long, grey arms wrapped themselves around Lewis. His chest creaked.

Lewis screamed again.

The child smiled.

Squeezed.

Penny couldn't move.

Couldn't turn away.

She heard bones snap and Lewis' shrieks turn to chokes. Gargles. His face turned purple.

Black.

His chest grew smaller, thinner. The child squeezed and grinned, and pushed itself into him as blood began crawling out of his throat. He turned to Penny. Opened his mouth to speak.

Penny turned and fled.

Her footsteps echoed behind her as she ran.

Chapter Six

Penny's breath came out in great burning gasps. The sound of her footsteps pounding so loudly in her ears that she could not hear anything else. Not the wind or the trees or the sound of a pursuit.

She forced herself down the slope that led away from the cavern, towards the forest and the river, toeing the thin line between running and stumbling. Her injured foot sent shockwaves of pain up her leg.

The sensation spurred her on.

There was no way of knowing if the 'changed' creature would stay with Lewis, as the others did with their victims, or continue after her once it had finished. There was also no way to know if the light of the burning curtain had lured more of them to her location.

All she knew was that whether she was being followed or not, she needed to keep running. To get away. Or her foot could soon be the least of her concerns.

She could see the river peeking through the trees below. If she could reach it and get to the other side, perhaps she would be safe. Perhaps she could get away.

Penny grunted as she pushed forward.

She clambered over rocks, ducking under branches thick with amber leaves that came away as she crashed into them. The river sparkled before her.

'I'll make it,' she gasped. 'I'll make it.'

She bounded over another rock, sharp and pointed, but fell short. Her wounded foot hit the peak and scraped along it. Penny screamed – an awful sound that became a cry and then a gag. She rolled and fell to the floor. Dirt filled her mouth and her eyes overflowed with tears.

She shuddered and vomit burned inside her throat. Nothing could hold it back and, shoulders lurching, she threw up where she lay. When the heaves had subsided, Penny pushed her fist into her mouth and bit down, trembling.

She couldn't get up in time. She couldn't run.

She was going to die.

She closed her eyes and trembled in the dirt.

She was going to die.

Something was rustling behind her. She could hear branches snap.

She was going to die.

She was going to die.

Stay still, she told herself. *It's blind in the daylight. Just stay still.*

Don't move. Don't make a sound. Just stay still. Think about something else.

Mary.

Think about Mary.

Penny breathed deeply. In and out. There was no forest in her mind. No creature with small, grasping hands. Just herself. Turning up at Mary's door. Snatching her son away. Watching Mary cry. Drinking in the look on Mary's face when she had caught her with Lewis.

Lewis turning purple, grey hands around his chest.

A closed door. A dark room.

Pounding.

Mary dead.

Mary dead.

Mary dead.

Grass rustled, close to her ear.

Penny sobbed but her cries made no sound. Made no mark.

She had no tears left.

She was so tired of this.

Running.

Hiding.

Crying.

Big girls don't cry, Pen.

Chin up.

She needed to survive, needed to get Mary away from her son.

I hate her, Penny thought. *I hate her. I just want to go home.*

A musical chirping sounded close by and Penny lifted her head just enough to see above the dirt.

A little brown bird hopped a few metres away, cocking his head and whistling. It was impossible and stupid, but Penny knew it was the same bird that had taunted her before. Her face filled with blood and shame.

It hopped closer, chirped again, mocking her.

Penny screamed at it and it flew off out of sight.

'Damn it, damn it, *damn it.*'

She moved her arms, placing them palm down either side of her head as if she were about to do a push up. She pulled her knees to her chest, sat up, and then forced herself to her feet. She wobbled, but refused to hold on to a tree.

She was sick of trees. Sick of this damn forest.

Penny walked.

She did not limp; she would not allow herself to limp. Instead, every time her wounded foot hit the ground she swore beneath her breath. While winding through the forest, Penny left a trail of curses mingled with the smell of sweat.

She grew dizzy.

Everything started to look the same and she could no longer see the river in front of her. Sometimes she would find herself facing a tree she had passed a few moments before. Had she made a wrong turn? Had she been mistaken about seeing the river before? Hallucinating in her panic? The river hadn't seemed that far from the cave, but she had been wandering for hours.

What did it matter if she had made a wrong turn? She could only keep going.

The trees became thicker. A wall of green. Penny could no longer duck and dive between branches, she had to climb through them.

The forest was fighting against her.

She pushed a shrub away from her face, and caught sight of something flat and smooth, shimmering faintly in the daylight.

The river.

She was so close.

A bramble caught at her jacket pocket. She grabbed and pulled until it came loose with a rip. Thorns entwined themselves in her hair.

Why was the river getting smaller?

Why wasn't it moving?

It was so still.

So calm.

So…

She stopped. Peering through the trees, she began to laugh, hysterically, clutching her stomach as it cramped with joy and hunger.

She pushed aside a low, fan-like branch, and stepped onto the flat grey surface in front of her. The grey stone sparkled as daylight bounced across it from above. The surface was clean and smooth, broken only by the encroaching roots that had started to claim the path as its own. Penny walked to its centre. It was warm against the soles of her feet.

She looked left and then right.

'Which way? Which way?' she mumbled.

To the left, the path wound upward, crumbling apart as it was overtaken by the trees on either side. The forest would keep her shaded and give her more places to hide.

Water rolls down, said a voice in her head.

The river would not be in that direction.

The path to her right was wide and open, with no cover or places to scurry out of sight. It continued for a short while, and then disappeared from view after a sharp downward slope.

Water rolls down.

Penny turned right.

She soon became grateful for the path for two reasons. First of all, the smooth surface made it much easier to walk on her increasingly painful foot. Second, the downward slope meant that she was able to see what was coming quicker than she would have been able to otherwise. If anything appeared below her, she would be able to run and hide before being seen.

Unfortunately, being on the path also meant that the canopy above her was thinner. When it started to rain, almost painfully hard, even her jacket couldn't stop her from getting wet. She pulled the hood tightly over her head, clinging on as the water sprayed her face.

It was too much.

Frustrated, Penny ran from the path and into the forest, hoping to find shelter beneath the limbs of a large, towering oak. She panted as she leaned against it, staring into the trees around her. Her eyes narrowed.

There was something deeper in the trees, a dark grey at odds with the greenery around it. Stone, it looked like, but much higher than any natural stone should have been.

Penny approached it with caution. When close enough to touch it, she reached out, brushing the stone with her fingers and running them over the rough surface. Tracing the cracks where concrete had once held bricks together.

A man-made wall.

A trace of humanity.

But what was it guarding?

She followed the wall down the slope, one hand against it, tracing the stones as she walked. The wall was crumbling near the top but not low enough for her to catch a glimpse of anything on the other side.

The dilapidation grew worse as she continued, the wall starting to fall apart in places. Soon Penny came across a gap in the stone, a hole large enough to squeeze through. With only a moment's thought and a quick glance over her shoulder, she went inside.

She wasn't sure what she had expected. Another version of the house perhaps, tall and stately. Maybe surrounded by farmland instead of trees and rocks. She supposed she had hoped for a small group of people, just one or two would have done. Somebody that she could have cried to and guilt-tripped into giving her some food or water.

Instead, set back behind large overgrown shrubs, was a small, broken-looking building, a house from before all the madness. It had collapsed under the pressure of the forest and the weight of its own roof, and lay shrunken and pathetic as it crumbled into the woodland. A large rope had been tied around the branches of a tree just off to one side of the house. The other end of the rope had been tied to a tyre.

Penny stepped back, suddenly very aware of where she was.

This had been a private home. A private home that, very likely, had housed a child who played on that tyre.

But, which type of child had it been home to?

Did the creatures ever remain near the homes they had once known?

Penny turned her ear to the sky, but the rain had started again a little while back, and there was no way of hearing any birdsong through it. Or lack thereof. She looked back behind her, towards the path. If she didn't stay here, she would have to keep going and hope that the rain would ease off before she needed to find a place to sleep. If it didn't, this house would be her best option for shelter through the night.

There was still quite a while until nightfall, though Penny had no real way of knowing what time it was. She could still leave now. Find somewhere else.

Penny bit her lip, and then looked back at the house.

It would be a wasted opportunity if she didn't at least check out the building, wouldn't it? There could be food inside. Dry clothes.

It's what her father would have done, wasn't it?

Penny groaned quietly and began walking towards the house.

As she got closer, she realised that the building was smaller than she had first thought. It couldn't have been home to many people at all, and had two or three rooms at best. This fact made her feel safer as she stopped in front of the little house, but not by much.

The exterior walls might have been white once, but were now so thickly covered in dried dirt it was hard to tell. Vines snaked their way up the walls and Penny pulled at them, hands wrapped in the sleeves of her jacket, just in case they turned out to be poisonous. Another trick her father had taught her.

Soon enough she found what had once been the door. It lay half-broken in its frame, open to the elements, but this allowed Penny to climb into the building without much trouble.

Inside, the house was overgrown with vegetation, and Penny might have thought she was back in the forest if it hadn't been for the thick walls that shielded her from the heavy rain. The floor was a peculiar carpet made up of stone, rubble and various plants. The ruins of an old sofa against one wall and the decayed fireplace opposite it were the only signs of past life that remained.

Penny stepped over the various debris, and through the only

door she could see into next room. It appeared to be a kitchen, still partially covered by the roof and almost untouched by the vegetation that had taken over next door. Several intact cabinets and shelving units were strewn about the walls, their doors closed. Sealed.

A possible goldmine.

She held her breath and waited, standing motionless as she scanned the room. Praying she was alone.

Twenty seconds.

Thirty.

Nothing.

She exhaled and allowed her shoulders to relax.

Time to get to work.

The first cupboard she opened was a huge disappointment, made up of a mountain of dust and plastic tubs. She placed the tubs to one side and reached into the cupboard, searching through the dust just to be sure.

Nothing.

The next cupboard was even worse. It was just a pile of wet, old cardboard that had once contained food, before something had burrowed into it. Next to the cardboard was a selection of various rusted pans and trays. Useless.

The third cupboard was better. A large assortment of unopened tins and jars. She pulled them all out one by one, sorting them into piles.

Tins of food that needed heating went in one pile. The tins and jars of things that had expired long ago Penny threw over her shoulder without thought. The most exciting pile was the third, which contained several round, airtight containers; plastic tubs filled with powders and dried goods. Food that was made to last.

She opened each of the sealed tubs in turn, looking for anything that wouldn't require heat or water to use. She licked her finger, pushing it into a few of the powders and tasting them. Most were awful and obviously expired, but a few of the sweeter powders seemed okay. She put these to one side.

Most of the jars turned out to be a bust, several green and mouldy at the centre, but one jar contained a beautiful golden goo that had

almost completely solidified. She opened it up and licked the lid. The
goo was sweet and sticky.

Honey.

She dunked her fingers into the honey and licked them clean, but
forced herself to put the jar away from reach in the good pile. As delicious as the honey was, she needed something of more substance right
now. She moved over to the tins and turned them about in her hands,
looking for pull-tabs and finding none.

'Damn it.'

She re-opened the cupboards she had already searched through,
this time looking for a knife or some sort of sharp object. Penny found
nothing.

She picked up a rock from the living room floor and tried smash-
ing it against a tin. It dented, but did not open.

She threw both tin and rock across the room, grunting.

This couldn't be everything there was. There had to be something she had missed.

Penny stood, her legs already shaking from overuse, and turned
about the room. In the far corner, close to what had once been a window, was a stream of vines cascading through the ceiling and covering the wall. Penny walked over, squinted, and pushed her hand into
the thick blanket of weeds. Her fingers ran over the smooth stone of
the wall behind until they reached a cold, thin object.

A hinge.

Penny ripped the vines from the wall, not caring enough to use
her jacket as protection.

A small wooden door was hidden beneath the green, painted the
same colour as the walls. No wonder she hadn't seen it before.

Hoping for a larder, Penny pulled at the handle, and when that
didn't work, she pushed. The door jerked slightly, but not enough.
She pushed harder, shoving against the door with her shoulder until it
slammed open.

The room beyond was a haze of dust and green shadows. A large
bed took up most of the room, rusted metal, the bedding decayed
except for a thick woollen blanket that lay across the top. Penny

wrapped it around herself and began to look through the wooden wardrobe beside the bed.

Inside was mostly a mess of moth-eaten pieces of fabric, but a pair of leather sandals made her smile. They were far too big for her, but she slipped them on anyway, pulling the straps tightly around her ankles. It was nice to have an extra layer between the floor and her poor feet, though her injured foot throbbed at its confinement.

Opposite the bed was a door, and she was making her way over to it when something caught her eye. A collapsed wooden structure at the base of the bed, crumpled and sad.

A cradle.

Slowly she walked over to it, flinching a little when she saw that something lay inside. Something brown and broken.

Penny leaned over, and pulled out the old collection of rusted metal and damaged wood. A baby's mobile. All the colours had chipped away, but it jangled a pretty lullaby as she lifted it. She smiled. Her son had liked bells as a baby. She had forgotten that.

Penny placed the mobile back into the crib and tried not to picture the child that had once lay below it. Or the child that had not. She moved away, throat catching.

A door on the far wall led to a once white, now yellowed, bathroom. There was no running water when she tried the taps, and a stale stench leaked from the exposed pipes in the wall. There was a cupboard above the sink, however, and Penny scrambled to open the box that she found within.

Bandages, medicine, any type of first aid kit would have been helpful. Instead, Penny found a sewing kit, a vial of liquid that reeked of flowers and alcohol, and a plastic bag. Penny took it all, disappointed, and returned to the kitchen.

She watched the daylight fade from the kitchen window as she sat cross-legged on the stone floor, wrapped in the blanket and licking at the jar of honey. She did not waste even the smallest drop, chasing the rivers of gold that ran across her hand with her tongue. She had placed a few tins, as well as the powders, into the plastic bag she found in the bathroom. When she tired of the sticky sweetness she put the honey away too, and began to sew up the holes in her jacket. She had never been good at sewing, though she tried her best and actually enjoyed it sometimes. It took her several minutes and a lot of cursing to re-thread the needle each time it came loose, which happened frequently. The stitches were chunky and crude, and they would have made her a laughing stock in the house, but it would save a lot of rain from reaching her skin. When she'd finished, and there was still a bit of light in the room, she started another project.

She pulled down the ragged living room curtains, and stitched them roughly together to make a poncho. Not a good one, of course. It was itchy, damp and smelled of rot, but it would be warmer than walking around in just her vest and the jacket, an extra layer against air that would be getting colder each day. Penny placed it over her head, needing to tug a little to get it over her ears.

Her stomach growled in anger and Penny wanted nothing more than to open up another jar and gorge herself. Instead, she curled up beneath the blanket, pushing herself deep into the corner of the room and away from the howling wind.

Penny was soon drowned in darkness as the last of the day vanished. Rain battered the trees around the house and dripped into the centre of the room. A drumming that should have been relaxing but only made her tense with each echoing thud. She placed a few of the plastic pots underneath the dripping, but they soon filled and overflowed. A trickle of water ran across the room, reaching Penny's toes. She pulled herself into a tight ball, arms around her knees, staring at nothing.

She closed her eyes.

With nothing else to distract her mind, Penny was forced to watch the scene from the morning play over and over again in her mind.

Creature moving.

Lewis screaming.

Turning to look at her.

Penny briefly wondered what he had been going to say to her, before falling into unconsciousness.

She did not dream.

Before #3

A single snowflake fell from the sky. It twirled in the air, spiralling, until it landed on the ground thick with ice. Penny shivered from more than the cold, and pulled her child, her baby, closer to her chest. He wriggled inside the thick blankets wrapped around them both, shuffling closer to her heat and placing a small hand against her skin.

The miracle child, they were calling him. The first child in twenty-seven years.

Since she had been born.

The gap seemed to be widening each time. Whatever had affected the world before everything had gone wrong, before... them, seemed to be getting worse. There had only been ten years between Mary and herself, but though many women were trying, none could conceive. None except for her.

Penny turned towards the river, and saw Mary standing beside it. Her face was as white as the chunks of ice that floated on the water, her lips tight.

Penny watched another snowflake fall. She would need to go inside soon. She couldn't be outside in the snow, not with her.

She pulled her son closer, cradling his head with her hand.

A small group of people appeared from behind the house, walking in silence as other people gathered around them and stared. Lewis stood in the centre of the crowd, dragging his boat behind him. Two elders stood on each side of him, looking at the ground. Their heavily lined faces looked solemn and uncomfortable.

The group walked through the crowd of bystanders, who parted for them. Penny stood at the front of the crowd. It wouldn't do to hide from this, not today. Lewis looked up at her as he passed and smiled at the baby in her arms. Penny instinctively pulled the child away, just a twitch, but enough for the woman beside her to notice. She placed a hand on Penny's elbow in comfort. Penny winced.

She hadn't meant to do that.

An elder placed his hand on Lewis' shoulder and pushed him

onward with a quick but firm shove. Out of the corner of her eye, Penny saw Mary's hand clench into a fist.

She almost pitied the woman.

The procession stopped at the water's edge. Lewis turned to one of the elders, smiling like a child. This seemed to unsettle the older man, who had to look at the others for support before starting his speech.

'Lewis Duncan. We can no longer ignore your crime. The child in Penelope's arms is clear proof of your crime against her. We must think about the safety of all in the house. You are no longer welcome here.'

Penny sensed the crowd's attention wander to her. Her cheeks grew hot but she did not look away, not even as her vision blurred with tears.

'I'm sorry for all this,' Lewis said, very matter of fact. 'I didn't realise what I did was so wrong.'

The crowd began to murmur. Several people gasped. A man on Penny's right shouted, 'I'll kill him' and others cheered in agreement. Somebody threw a rock, but it merely bounced off the boat beside Lewis and landed in the water.

Lewis turned to look at the crowd, confused but not angry. One of the elders pointed at the boat, her face pinched in anger.

'I think it is time for you to go.'

Lewis pushed the boat into the water and clambered inside. He sat, rather than lay, one arm clinging onto a rock on the riverside. He locked eyes with Penny. She swallowed, though her mouth was dry.

'May I say goodbye?' he asked, though whether he was speaking about her or her son she couldn't decide.

A man nearby, she couldn't see who, stepped forward as she looked at the ground.

'If he doesn't go now I'll get rid of him myself.'

More jeers from the crowd.

Penny stole a look through her eyelashes and caught the moment Lewis' face crumpled.

'Oh,' he said, 'very well.'

He removed his hand from the boulder. The boat rocked once, and then was still as the current began pulling it along.

'I love you,' he said, eyes on Penny. Snow was beginning to fall at speed now, a dizzying swirl. She took one last look at the man on the boat, pulled her child closer to her chest, and then turned away.

She couldn't bear it anymore.

Penny walked away from the river and rounded a corner out of sight. She moved quickly towards the entrance and carefully climbed up the slippery stone steps to the front door.

It was not much warmer inside, the stone walls seemed to absorb the cold, but at least there was no snow. Penny sighed and wiped away a melted snowflake from her son's face.

Footsteps rushed up behind her and Penny was pulled around by the shoulder. She was unable to do anything with the child in her arms, and so stood, calmly, as Mary threw her arm back and slapped her. There was a dull crack as her hand met Penny's cheek, leaving behind pins and needles.

Penny blinked, but did not say a word. Mary was shaking with rage, her brown hair flat against her face, weighed down by the damp snow.

'This is all your fault,' she said, lips hardly moving. 'This is all your fault.'

Penny, again, said nothing. Mary flushed an ugly shade of red and took a step closer.

'Don't you know what you've done?'

'Don't you know what you're *doing*?'

'You sent him away.'

'No, they did. I had no say in this at all.'

'He never touched you. Not like that. Go back out there and tell them. Tell them what happened!'

Not without a bitter smile, Penny began to bounce her son in her arms. Mary stepped forward again.

'You did all of this on purpose. You've killed him. Because of you, my husband is dead.'

'He hasn't been your husband for a long time.'

'Go out there and stop this, now!'

'I'm afraid I can't,' said Penny, shrugging. And then, with as much malice as she could muster, she spat, 'I don't think I'll be able to open the door.'

Mary turned pale.

'All of this. Everything. Because of a mistake I made all those years ago?'

Penny said nothing, and Mary stepped back, shaking her head.

'You've gone way too far. You've killed my husband.'

'It must be awful to lose someone you love that much.'

Mary flinched.

Satisfied, Penny turned her back on the little woman and kissed her son on the nose.

From behind, Mary let out a strangled cry.

Penny hoped the snow wouldn't settle.

Chapter Seven

The room was still thick with darkness when Penny woke, gasping and reaching out for her foot.

At first she thought there was something digging into the wound, that she had pressed something into it as she slept. Something sharp. She brushed at her foot to remove whatever was causing the pain, but there was nothing to brush away. Her foot spasmed against her touch, and the skin burned against her fingers.

Penny searched for her bandage and found it, warm and damp, almost sticky. She must have started bleeding again in the night. Penny swung her leg around until it was beneath the meagre light leaking in from the open window and then twisted her foot until she could just about see the bandage. There was no sign of blood. With a light hand, Penny placed her finger against the wound and then brought her fingers to her nose. It didn't smell like blood.

It smelled wrong.

There was nothing she could do until first light. Penny pushed herself up against the wall and stared at the branches beyond the window. She counted them over and over, hoping the repetition would bore her back to sleep.

Sleep did not come, and Penny spent the rest of the long night waiting for the shadows to fade.

She was stiff with the cold by the time the first beam of sunlight slid into the room, and her joints clicked as she wobbled to her feet. She felt twenty years older.

Penny stumbled across the room, half limping, grabbing a plastic tub of rainwater as she dragged her body into the sun and sunk to the floor beside the small rectangle of morning. She placed her foot into the light and her skin gleamed orange in the sun. Biting her lip, she tore off the sandal and started to peel the bandage away from her skin. It stuck in places, and Penny had to wet the fabric with the rainwater to get it off without taking pieces of skin with it. When she finished, she let the bandage fall to the floor, and lifted her foot into the air, towards her face.

She winced, and groaned quietly.

The wound, a gash across the arch of her foot, was a dark, angry red, the skin around it tight like a pimple. Yellow liquid seeped out of the wound itself, smelling like a dry mouth tastes.

Penny gulped down a few mouthfuls of the water, and then dipped her hand into the tub. The water wasn't clean, and speckles of something brown floated across the surface, but it was all she had. Gently she wiped away the pus and gunk, going slower when closer to the wound itself.

She recalled a time similar to this, back when her father had been alive. Wanting to impress him, Penny had tried balancing on the banister of the main staircase. She was doing well and called out for him to look, but just as he rounded the corner into view her leg wobbled, and she tumbled over the side. Luckily she had landed on the stairs and not onto the ground floor several long metres below. Once her father had dried her tears, he sat her down, lecturing her as he cleaned up her cuts and scrapes.

'You have to be careful,' he had said, taking a cloth and dousing it with something that stank of alcohol. 'We don't have much medicine here. What happens if someone is badly hurt, but there's no medicine for them because you used it all jumping out of trees or balancing on banisters?'

'I don't know,' Penny mumbled, staring at the ground.

Penny's father had sighed, and then placed his large warm hand against her cheek.

'Pen, you have to keep people on your side. You'll need them to help you one day. Hold still now, baby. This will hurt, but it will stop you getting infected.'

Penny had not cried as her father dabbed the alcohol against her skin. She was a big girl, and big girls don't cry.

Penny hissed as her fingernail scratched her foot, and then she paused.

Alcohol.

She remembered now. Back at the house they had kept bottles of clear alcohol in the basement for medical emergencies. After her accident, Penny's father had traded several woollen blankets for a whole bottle of the stuff.

'Always good to keep one on hand,' he had said.

What harm could there be in trying?

She stretched out across the room, fingers grazing the plastic bag crumpled in the far corner. With a bit of effort, Penny managed to drag the bag closer to her and pulled out the small clear vial of scented liquid. There wasn't much of it, but hopefully she wouldn't need it for very long.

Penny pulled off her jacket and stuffed the sleeve into her mouth. She gagged as her tongue was pushed back by the rotten smelling fabric, but clamped her teeth down anyway.

She opened the vial of liquid and poured it carefully over the wound.

The jacket did not stop her from screaming.

Jaw clenched and eyes streaming, Penny shrieked like a dying animal as the alcohol hit open flesh. She twitched and moaned, her whole body shaking with pain. When her foot stopped burning and she had wiped her eyes, she spat the fabric out of her mouth.

If nothing else, it had stopped her biting her tongue.

After a few deep breaths, Penny took another gulp of water and then washed the bandage in what remained. The water turned a sickly brown. Wincing, Penny re-tied the wet bandage around her foot. It wasn't as neat as it had been, but it was good enough. With effort, she managed to squeeze her foot back into the sandal.

She ate some more honey, making sure to leave as much as she could, and then collected the remaining tubs of water. She pushed the lids down hard. It was unlikely they would survive until she reached the river, but she wanted to try at least. Anything was worth trying at this point.

Putting the jacket back on was hard work, her arms still stiff from the days before, but she managed to shrug it on in the end. She covered her head with the blanket, wrapping it once around her neck to keep it from dangling. It scratched at her cheek, but was warm. Even without looking into a mirror she knew she looked ridiculous, but it would have to do. She collected her bag of food, placed the water inside, and made her way out of the house.

The air outside was fresh, delicious against her skin, and much, much colder. She limped onto the path, feeling better for having the sandals even though they rubbed her feet and pushed against her injury. The grass tickled her toes as she walked.

Rather than leaving through the hole in the wall, Penny followed a winding path around the house, a path that was more green than grey and more grass than stone. It crunched as she walked and guided her to a rusted metal gate set into the wall.

It opened with a scream.

Penny squeezed herself through a small gap, not wanting to prolong the sound.

She went on.

The path continued beyond the gate and she followed it, snaking through grass as high as her calves. Soon it began to widen and, before she knew it, had merged with the path from yesterday.

She continued onward down the slope.

Her sandals clapped against the ground, echoing in the still morning air.

Despite the wind creeping into hidden holes in her jacket, Penny was slick with sweat. The cracked stone beneath her feet seemed never ending, and though it was flat and easy to walk on, after several hours her legs were aching terribly. Several times the path turned a corner, and she willed the river to appear before her as she turned also.

It never did.

There was only the path and the trees.

The forest loomed on either side of her. She could see ahead, quite clearly, and would know if anything was approaching. But there was always movement within the forest: branches snapping, leaves rustling, the strange cries of wild animals.

Penny felt exposed.

Watched.

The plastic bag at her side rustled like frosted leaves with every breath she took. She might as well have been screaming out her location. Anybody could have heard her. Any*thing*. A creature could be nearby, hidden behind a tree. Waiting for someone to pass by. Arms outstretched. Grasping.

Penny bit her lip, staring nervously at a crooked branch as a beam of sunlight hit it momentarily, before casting it back into the shadows.

Had it been a branch?

Or an arm?

She didn't stop, didn't look back. If she stopped the fear might root her to the ground. Lock her into place.

She couldn't afford to keep still.

She saw Lewis in her mind. His face purple and his mouth open.

Penny walked clumsily onward, tripping over a loose rock. Stones clattered, but didn't the sound go on for a little too long?

Was someone, something, there?

Her skin prickled with unease.

She was uneasier still when she rounded the corner.

Trees parted like a flower opening in the spring, and Penny got her first good look at the path's destination. At the bottom of a steep hill, almost hidden in a field of long, thin grass, was a scattering of buildings.

A village.

Penny's stomach churned.

She turned and looked over her shoulder, back towards the forest. She would be safer going back.

Much, much safer.

Villages meant homes; homes meant people.

Penny was faced with the same question from yesterday, but this time it was much more potent.

Did the creatures remain near the homes they had once inhabited?

She turned back to look at the village. There was no reason at all to go near it. She had enough food for now, and even if her foot got worse, she could manage. She could force herself on.

There wasn't any sign of the river nearby at all, therefore there was no reason to stay.

She must have missed it on her way here. She needed to retrace her steps. If she entered the village, she would just be going backward.

Or worse.

Penny bit her lips again, this time drawing blood. She licked it as she thought through her options.

She had been walking for hours and, as there was no real way to tell the time, it could be getting dark soon. She shouldn't be wandering the forest in the dark. One of the houses could provide shelter. Besides, it would be a shame not to investigate, wouldn't it? She had said the same thing about the cottage after all, and that turned out to be perfectly safe.

'I'm going to die,' she said, wiping her nose on the back of her hand and continuing towards the buildings below.

Penny paused in front of a quaint stone house, weighing up her options as clouds drifted by, shadows against the rough ground.

The front door of the house was wide open, a waiting, welcoming mouth. The room beyond the doorway appeared full of light.

'Damn it,' she whispered, resigned.

Penny stepped over the threshold into the light, holding her bag close, hoping it would reduce the sound of rustling plastic but not really believing it. A flash of sunlight burned her eyes and she winced, stumbling blindly as she entered the room. She regained her balance, forced her eyes open and looked around.

A chill ran down her spine and it grew as her vision adjusted to the light.

She had made a mistake.

A horrible mistake.

The room was a disaster, anything that had once been of use torn off the walls or scratched to pieces. A mound of dirty fabric lay strewn across the floor alongside chunks of wood, some still wide enough for Penny to see claw marks. Large, deep claw marks.

Penny forced herself to breathe but instead of oxygen drew in a cloud of dust. Her breath caught in her chest and she struggled to hold in a coughing fit. She tensed her stomach to try to minimise the sound and did not breathe again until the coughs had subsided.

The sunlight from the door was warm against her back. It would be easy to turn around. To find another house, preferably one without teeth and claw marks.

But then again, what if the other houses were worse? What if the thing wasn't in here, waiting for Penny in a dark corner, but there?

It would be better to leave the village.

Run far, far away.

Penny chewed at her flaking lips, looked over her shoulder briefly, and then forced herself deeper into the house.

The following room was not much better. It had been a kitchen, once. Thick wooden cupboards lined a wall, the doors open and hanging from their hinges. A table lay on its side in the centre of the room, broken and covered in a sheet of dust.

Opposite her was a narrow staircase that dissolved into shadows the higher it went. Everything in the cupboards had been cleared out a long time ago; there was no point looking there. She would have more luck finding clothes or blankets upstairs. Penny hopped over a collection of old jars smashed on the floor, the glass clean. Useless.

She stood before the staircase, and arched her neck until she was staring up towards the second floor.

She could see nothing.

Gently she placed her foot on the first step, ready to pull away the instant she heard a creak. The staircase remained silent, and Penny continued her ascent.

The scratches soon became visible again. Claw marks marred each of the wooden steps, as if something had moved across them in a hurry. She wanted to turn back more than anything, but something pulled at her gut, urging her on. There had to be something she could use. Something to make this worthwhile.

As the second floor came into view, Penny could see more scratches, but this time they weren't on the floor.

They were on the walls.

On the doors.

The hair on her neck stood on end as her eyes darted to a black shadow at the far end of the hall. The shadow heaved.

It was moving.

Awake.

Her hands began to sweat.

In the stillness, Penny could hear breaths that were not her own.

She needed to turn back.

It would see her.

It was too close.

Far too close.

She needed to turn back now.

Eyes fixed on the darkness in front, Penny placed her foot behind her.

The staircase creaked.

Something snorted. A wet, angry sound.

There was no point being quiet now.

It had heard her.

Penny turned.

Ran.

She took the steps two at a time, the stairs betraying her every movement with screeches and thumps. Behind her she could hear scratching, snorting. Louder, faster, as the thing came closer.

And closer.

Within arm's reach.

Penny wailed as she stumbled out of the open doorway, her bag catching on a piece of wood and yanking her back. She fell to one knee, heard the thing near the door, and threw her arms around her head to protect her face.

Her breath echoed, caught in the fabric of her jacket.

Nothing was happening.

Why wasn't anything happening?

For the third time in almost as many days, Penny lowered her arms to look at the creature she had fled from.

Her face grew hot and her eyes stung in embarrassment.

In the doorway, staring at her with dark brown eyes was a thin, dirty dog. Its hair was grey and straggly, clumped together with mud and matted fur. Its face was flat, squat, with dark marks around its nose and snout. It snorted at her, as if questioning why she had woken it from its sleep.

Face burning, Penny grabbed a handful of small rocks and threw them at the doorway. The dog did not flinch, didn't even blink.

Penny glared at it.

'Stupid dog. You fucking stupid dog. Go away, go on!'

The dog snorted again. Penny threw more rocks, growing more and more frustrated as each one missed. One rock bounced off the door frame and hit the dog's paw. The dog bent down and sniffed, then rose to its feet. It walked past her, tail raised, and disappeared behind another building.

Penny lowered her head onto her knees and exhaled.

There was no way she'd be able to go back in the house now, not even with the dog gone. Something that she pretended was fear, but was more like shame, held her back. Instead, Penny rose to her feet and made her way deeper into the village, drawing her jacket closer as the sunlight fell behind a dark cloud.

She needed somewhere safe to rest and work out what to do next. Somewhere unlikely to be home to any creature of the forest, be that a nightmarish monster or a four-legged mongrel that would chase her down the stairs.

A place where she could find food.

She came to a stop in front of a small building covered in what looked like a metal shutter. A sign above the curtain read 'Al's General Store'.

She knew what 'store' meant, all right.

Penny smiled.

The metal shutter, full of holes like a net, covered the entire front of the building. Penny peered into one of the holes, hands cupped either side of her face until the interior came into view.

The window was covered in a layer of dust, streaked like mud across the glass. But now and then there was a small gap of clarity, through which Penny could see shelves full of boxes and cans. Almost entirely untouched.

She stepped back, pushed her fingers into one of the holes and shook the shutter. It rattled like thunder and Penny winced as the noise echoed. When nothing happened, she frowned and tried again.

The shutter moved, just slightly, but nowhere near enough to get inside.

She kicked the metal and it clanged. The noise echoed and faded again, but this time the silence that followed was different. There was a trace of something else in the air, almost a hum.

Penny stiffened as a warm hand wrapped itself around her wrist and something cold was pressed against her throat.

'If you make one more sound,' said a venomous voice in her ear, 'I'll take this knife and gut you.'

Chapter Eight

Penny was at a loss for what to say; the surprise, and the knife at her throat, did well to render her speechless. A hand patted her down, feeling for lumps in her clothing, and then snatched the plastic bag from Penny's hand.

Penny cried out, stopping only when the knife was pushed, firmly, into her neck.

'I didn't tell you to speak. Be quiet.'

Penny clamped her mouth shut and glared at the space in front of her.

The bag rustled for a moment, quickly. Something trickled down Penny's neck. Sweat or blood.

'Where did you get this?' asked the voice. It was deep and raw, barely used.

Penny said nothing and continued to glare.

The person behind her sighed.

'Fine. Look, I'm going to turn you around, okay? But you have to be quiet. You've made too much of a racket already and there is too little sun today for all of that noise. You need to be quiet. Do you understand?'

Penny nodded.

She flexed her hands, ready to turn and defend herself.

The pressure of the knife fell away from her neck, and firm hands grasped her shoulders, turning her. Penny snarled, ready to pounce, faltering at the last moment.

She had expected a man from the roughness of the voice, but the gangly woman in front of her was a total surprise. In her shock, Penny's arms dropped to her sides, empty of their thirst for revenge. The woman watched Penny, wary, dark eyes searching every part of her. Examining her. Penny hunched back instinctively.

The woman held up the plastic bag of food with one hand, and pointed the knife at Penny with the other. It was not a threatening movement, but one that told Penny she would have to do as she was told.

'Where did you get this?' she asked again.

Penny found her anger once more.

Why should she defend herself? She had done nothing wrong. She scowled.

'Why should I tell you? You're going to take it from me anyway.'

The woman edged closer, the knife glinting.

'Who gave this to you? I need to know.'

'Well that's a shame, isn't it?'

The woman stepped forward. This time the threat was clear. Penny half rolled her eyes.

'Oh, calm down. I found it. Nobody gave me anything.'

The woman came closer again. For a brief moment sunlight escaped from its cloudy prison, and Penny could see the many lines etched into the woman's face. Scars carved by a hard life.

The woman considered what Penny had told her, furrowing her brows.

'Nobody gave you this? You're sure?'

'Of course I'm sure. I think I'd remember something like that.'

'Where are the others in your group?'

'What others?'

This time it was the woman who rolled her eyes.

'You can't survive alone. Not out here. There are too many false ones that hide in the woods nearby.'

'There are more people with you? Here?' Penny asked. The woman waved the question away with her free hand, as if swatting a fly.

'I said that *you* couldn't survive alone. I didn't say that I couldn't. Your group, where are they? Will they be coming here?'

'It's just me.'

There was a moment of silence. The woman stared, mouth twitching, as if she wanted to laugh.

How dare she laugh, after all Penny had been through?

'You think that's funny?' said Penny, spitting out the words like pins and needles. The woman tensed but said nothing.

So she was too good to speak to her now. Well, knife or not, Penny would never be looked down on.

She reached forward and grabbed the woman's wrist. The knife wavered in the air in front of Penny as the women fought for control, but she did not look at it. She lowered herself to the woman's height, leaning forward until she could smell her sweat.

'Don't you dare laugh at me.'

To her left came a deep, menacing growl. Penny glared at the woman for a few more seconds, and pulled away. The dirty grey dog that had chased Penny down the stairs walked over to the other woman and sat at her feet. She placed her hand on its head to calm it, and then sighed loudly.

'Look, I'm sorry. If you don't want to tell me how you actually got here, that's fine. I'm not all that interested.'

Penny opened her mouth to speak but the woman held up her hand.

'Don't,' she said. 'Keep it to yourself. Just… did you see anyone on your way here? A young woman, maybe your age. She looks like me. Have you seen anyone?'

'No,' said Penny. She didn't feel bad for lying. She doubted the other woman wanted to know about Lewis.

The woman closed her eyes, wincing as if in deep pain. She drew in a breath, exhaled, and pushed her knife into a hole made in her belt.

'Thank you,' she said, opening her eyes at last. 'You can go now.'

She threw the plastic bag onto the floor, and started to walk briskly back around the building with the dirty-looking dog at her heels. Penny gaped, and then followed.

'Hey, wait.'

The woman did not turn around.

'You need to go,' she called out over her shoulder. 'You've already made too much noise and the sun won't be out for much longer. The false ones will be here soon.'

'You think I don't know that? Listen, I need to get back to the river. You need to show me where it is.'

'I do not need to do anything at all.'

Growling, Penny limped forward at speed, grabbed the woman by the shoulder and turned her around.

They were close to a chain-link fence that surrounded the back of the store. Penny shoved the woman into it and the metal squeaked. The dog began to snarl.

'I need to get back to my son, and I need to get back to him immediately. You have to tell me where the river is.'

The woman stared at her, barely moving.

'You have a son?' she asked, under her breath.

'Yes, magic, I know. You've got to know where the river is. You have to show me. Please.'

The woman slowly moved her gaze from Penny and towards the sky.

'The clouds are too thick today. The sun is gone,' she said, then pushed Penny away with an alarming strength. Penny stumbled back, landing awkwardly on her foot and hissing. The woman lifted an area of the fence and the dog ran through the gap.

'We need to get inside,' she said. 'They'll be here soon. Hurry up.'

The woman led Penny through a small hole in the back door of the building. It was a tight squeeze, but the growing silence creeping up behind gave her an added push. As soon as she was through the door, the woman began shoving a large wooden box over the hole to block the gap.

Despite the daylight outside, the room was almost entirely black. Thick cardboard lined the windows, blocking every nook and cranny. It seemed to be a small storage room, but Penny didn't have much time to look before the box covered the last of the hole, removing all trace of light.

'I can't see anything,' Penny said, holding out an arm as if to touch the darkness.

'Shh,' said the woman. Penny felt something being pushed into her hands and grabbed it. A rope.

'Follow,' said the woman in a whisper, and tugged on the rope.

Penny began to walk, guided by the pulling of the rope. It took two hands to be able to follow properly, to know if the rope had changed direction. At one point, she fell into something solid, thumping against it loudly enough that the woman jerked the rope in anger.

She passed through what felt like an open doorway. The rope went limp, and from behind came the sound of a door swinging to a close.

'You may talk now,' said the woman. 'But quietly. They hear better than you might think.'

'I can't see a damn thing. Where are you?'

'Close by. Wait a moment.'

Something buzzed and clanked, a plastic sound. A thin, yellow stream of watery light slowly grew in size until the thick inky darkness became just a thin shadowy veil. The woman was leaning against a stone wall, smiling slightly and holding an old, wind-up torch. The dog lay at her feet. She waved the torch, making the shadows of the room dance.

'It comes in handy. Not bright enough to escape through any cracks, but enough to see by.' She placed the torch on a shelf, and then sank onto an uncomfortable-looking sofa. She gestured about the room.

'Make yourself at home.'

Penny frowned. The room was claustrophobic, littered with old boxes and discarded plastic wrappers. The only piece of furniture was the sofa, square and rotted. A door in front of her led to what Penny guessed was the storefront she had seen from outside. The whole place smelled unpleasantly of damp and urine.

'I don't understand,' she said.

The woman smiled slightly.

'What do you not understand?'

'You were ready to gut me ten minutes ago, now you want me to get comfortable?'

The woman shrugged, a lock of thick hair falling across her face.

'I'm not a monster. If you had stayed outside, you wouldn't have made it. As I said, many false ones hide in these woods. The buildings must remind them of people. Frightening, isn't it? Thinking of them as being able to remember.'

'If there are that many of them here how have you survived?'

'Like a rat,' said the woman. 'Much like you have, I imagine.'

Penny swallowed a retort like bile.

'Right, well, thank you for the offer but I really need to leave.'

'Feel free. Like I said, you won't make it. Not until tomorrow morning, at least.'

'I've made it this far, haven't I?'

The woman shrugged again. Exasperated, Penny sank to the floor. Her foot throbbed in gratitude.

They sat in silence for a long time, the air scented with foul smells and awkwardness. Penny shuffled, uncomfortable, trying to stretch her foot to ease the pain. The light began to dim, but the woman rose only when it had vanished completely. She wound the torch, and then went back to her seat. Penny tucked her foot under her, not wanting the woman to see as she passed, but bringing attention upon herself by moving.

'Are you injured?' she asked, frowning slightly.

'It's fine,' said Penny.

'You look as though you're in a lot of pain. May I see?'

'It's fine,' Penny said again, but the woman was already kneeling in front of her, hand outstretched.

'Do you always threaten your guests and then treat their injuries?'

'Just the pretty ones,' said the woman, smiling.

Penny scowled, but stuck out her foot for inspection. The woman gently removed the sandal and unwound the bandage, wrinkling her nose.

'What on earth did you do?'

'Scratched it.'

'It's infected.'

'I know.'

The woman sighed and stood. She rummaged around a shelf, pulling out a small box from behind an old book. She kneeled again, opened the box and pulled out strips of fabric and a small bottle of white liquid.

The sting of the alcohol against her foot was nearly unbearable, but Penny forced herself to remain still and silent. She didn't want the woman to hear her scream.

The woman finished, re-wrapped Penny's foot with the fresh fabric and sat back.

'What's your name?' she asked, wiping her hands on her shirt.

Penny thought about giving a false name, if only out of childish spite, but didn't have the energy.

'Penelope,' she said.

'I'm Samantha. Let's get you something to eat, you must be very hungry.'

Without waiting for a reply, Samantha crept into the next room, leaving Penny alone with the dog. The dog snorted at her, obviously as happy with the situation as she was.

'Don't look at me like that,' she muttered. 'I don't even want to be here.'

The dog snorted again.

Samantha returned, carrying several large tins. She sat, pulled out her knife and sawed into the metal to remove the lid. She handed a tin to Penny.

'It's meat,' Samantha said, laughing quietly as Penny stared at the mushy pink contents of the tin. 'Though I don't know what. The labels have all rubbed off now. It tastes fine.' She dumped half of her tin on the floor for the dog, and then scooped a handful of the mince into her mouth.

Penny's hunger and repulsion had a quick confrontation, but hunger won almost instantly. She began shovelling the food into her mouth, stopping only to breathe. The mince was salty, and the texture was difficult to describe. In some places, it felt almost like frog spawn in her mouth.

She gagged at the image, but refused to surrender the food.

Samantha was watching her again, and Penny shifted on the floor, avoiding her eyes.

'So,' said Samantha, 'if you aren't out here with a group, how have you survived?'

'Does it matter?' said Penny, in between mouthfuls.

'I suppose not. I'm just curious. Could you not satisfy my curiosity, in exchange for the food?'

A small thought flickered at the back of Penny's mind. She swallowed the food, and then smiled.

'How about you tell me how I can get back to the river, then I tell you how I got here?'

Samantha laughed, her voice raspy.

'We'll talk about the river soon enough, and discuss your payment for *that* information then. First, the food. Consider your stay here tonight complimentary.'

It took a lot of effort to keep her smile from fading, but Penny just about managed it. It was easier to fake a friendly face when you needed something.

'Fine,' she said, and leaned back. 'I was left here a few days ago. Someone… someone in my safe house didn't like me. They tried to kill me. Put me on a boat and sent me down the river. She has my son now, and I need to get back to him. Can you help me?'

'A few days,' said Samantha, sighing. 'I see. You wouldn't have seen her then.'

Always take an interest in others, her father said in her mind.

People are always more receptive when they think you care for them, Penny thought.

'Who?' asked Penny.

Samantha stared at her, her dark brown eyes almost black in the shadows.

'My sister. She went missing two weeks ago.'

'I'm sorry,' said Penny, gently, as if speaking to a child. 'I wish I could help.'

Samantha smiled.

'I'm glad you've said that. I want you to bring her back to me.'

Chapter Nine

Penny's initial reaction was laughter, but this quickly faltered as she noticed Samantha's stern, unchanging expression.

'Look,' Penny said, brushing back her hair, 'I'm very happy you didn't gut me and that you're letting me hide here for the night, but I need to get back to my son.'

'And I need to find my sister.'

'I don't have a lot of time. If I don't get back soon I won't be able to get back at all. I can't afford to help you. I'm sorry, but I can't. I don't have time to wander about searching for a missing woman.'

Samantha stared at her in the dim light, calm.

'You will never find the river without me. You will never make it back to your son. These woods are almost impossible to navigate. I can take you to the river, but you need to help me get my sister first.'

'Get your sister? What do you mean, "get" your sister? You said she was missing.'

Samantha looked at the floor.

'She is. I believe she's being held against her will.'

'Kidnapped? You think that out there, in that damn forest, there are not just other people who have survived, but a gang of kidnappers?'

Penny laughed again. Samantha slammed a fist against the wall, her nostrils flaring. The dog whined and put its head on her lap.

'I know she was taken. I know. She went out to talk some sense into those... she went out to see them. To bring them food. She did not come back.'

'There are others out there? How many of you are hiding in this damn place?'

Samantha glared and took a calming breath.

'There were four of us who left the camp. We were tired of the people there. We were a novelty to them, my sister and I. The pretty women with the dark skin. We were safer on our own.'

She began scratching at the paint on the wall. It crumbled to the ground like stained snow. Penny winced, suddenly feeling very sick.

'The other two,' Samantha continued, unaware of Penny's discomfort, 'were an older couple. They joined the camp late, only a few months ago, and I never asked their names. They liked to keep to themselves. I heard rumours though. People called them witches, demon worshippers. Some said they had been doctors, back before everything changed. They heard we were leaving and wanted to come along. They said they wanted a fresh start. I was... uncomfortable, but Rose, my sister, she trusted them. So we left together.'

'Why aren't they here with you, if you all left together?'

A small gust of wind shrieked through a gap in the door.

'We... stopped at a small cottage. Near here. We were comfortable but things started happening. Strange things. I would catch the ends of peculiar conversations, or see them watching Rose from afar. They didn't like me, but they loved Rose. I... saw the woman standing over Rose's bed when I awoke one evening. We left soon afterwards, without them. That must have been around a month ago, now.'

'Right,' said Penny, unsure of what else to say. 'Okay. That is creepy, but why would you think they had kidnapped her?'

'They were obsessed!' Samantha shouted, loud enough to startle the dog. 'They were distraught when we left. Ranting about her youth, her vitality. They wanted something from her, I know it.'

'Then why the hell did you let her go to see them?'

The words had left Penny's mouth before she had time to censor them. Samantha dug her nails into her thigh.

'I didn't. A few weeks ago, Rose said that she had spoken to one of them on the outskirts of town. She said they were starving, that they needed help. I refused to do anything, and so one morning, before I had awoken, she left. She had left me a note, told me she would be back before evening. She was not. I would never have let her put herself in danger like that. Especially not for them.'

The light dimmed down to nothing once more. This time Penny stood and wound the torch, wanting something to occupy her hands. When she could see again, she found Samantha bent over her knees, her head in her hands.

'Look,' Penny said, feeling a little bad for the woman. 'I under-

stand how you feel, I do. But I can't afford to go off looking for someone who probably isn't alive. You know it's more likely that one of
those things found her, don't you?'

'The couple have her. I know it.'

'Okay, fine. Let's say that they do. What exactly am I supposed
to do? I'm at a bit of a disadvantage here.' Penny gestured to her foot.
Samantha caught her eyes and held her gaze.

'They would never let me near the cottage. They know me,
would know what I was trying to do. But they don't know you and
you're younger than I am. They'll like that. They will think you
naive. Trusting. Once you're inside, you just need to find her and get
her out.'

'You make it sound easy.'

The woman stared at her, and Penny looked away under the
weight of her gaze.

'I'm sorry,' she said. 'I am. But it's not going to happen. Just let
me leave now, I'll get out of your way.'

'You'll never find the river without me.'

'Well, I've made it this far.'

Penny stood, limping towards the door. Samantha chased after
her, frantic. The dog began to whine.

'Please,' she cried. 'I'm begging you. Help me find her and I'll get
you to your son. I promise.'

Penny was close to the door. The light was fading again; she
must not have wound the torch properly.

'I'm leaving, I'll find somewhere else to shelter for the—'

A large crash echoed from beyond the next room and both
women froze.

The dog barked.

The air was still.

Penny placed one hand on the door handle, only for Samantha to
grab her wrist and pull her away. Penny did not resist.

'It heard us,' Samantha whispered. 'It heard us shouting.'

Penny shivered and looked up towards the door. Behind the
frosted glass window was a shadow, small and childlike. A hand
reached up and pressed against it.

'Haaaa.'

The dog whined and trembled.

Penny felt sick.

How could they have been so stupid?

So loud?

Samantha's grip was tight around her wrist, urging her to move.

Penny stepped back, slowly.

The shadow moved also.

'Haaaa.'

'It will see us,' Penny whispered, barely a breath. Samantha's lips trembled but her chin was high. She began to lean to one side, arm outstretched in the dimness.

'When I say so,' she whispered, eyes never moving from the door, 'move to the side of the door. Nod if you understand me.'

Penny nodded. Samantha nodded also, but seemingly to herself, rather than in reply. With one hand, she grasped the plastic torch Penny had left on the wooden shelf. With the other, she wrapped her hand around the dog's collar.

The women breathed in unison, preparing themselves. Penny had no idea what Samantha was going to do, but she knew that she wouldn't like it. Her mind was filled with visions, of grey hands around her neck. Of vicious smiles and screams in the dark.

'Okay,' Samantha said. 'Start moving now. Slowly, do not make quick movements.'

Penny started to edge towards the door. Each step felt like a lifetime, she wasn't even sure if she was moving quickly or slowly.

Time stood still.

She could feel the creature watching her behind the glass. Could picture its wet, black eyes upon her.

She started to sweat.

Penny's hand brushed against cool stone. She had reached the wall. Carefully she turned and pressed her back against it. The door was no longer in sight, but the dim light from the window cast a thin, distorted shadow on the opposite wall. Somehow it was worse than seeing the creature directly.

How had they not noticed it before?

Penny turned to Samantha, who had grown pale.

'I am going to throw the torch,' Samantha said. 'When I do, you need to run. Do you understand?'

'*What?*'

'Do you understand?'

Penny nodded, heart throbbing in her throat. Samantha nodded back. She pressed the torch, light side against her stomach and began to crank it into life. Light spilled from the torch and Penny watched the shadow cock its head at an inhuman angle.

Penny could only hear the sound of her own heart.

Two beats of silence.

Three.

'Now,' Samantha yelled, and tossed the torch to the other side of the room.

Its light filled the air and for half a second everything was calm. Still.

Then the creature began to shriek.

The door was thrown off its hinges, a cloud of dust and wood, and a dark shape shot through it, faster than anything Penny had ever seen.

'Go!' Samantha screamed, already sounding distant. Penny pushed through the doorway. The previously dark room was illuminated with milky light.

A shriek from behind.

Penny looked over her shoulder, just quickly enough to catch a glimpse of the creature. It was hunched forward, gripping the torch and staring directly into the light.

Its skin was wet.

Grey.

Veins in its small hands stark against its skin.

The torch trembled in the thing's unhuman grasp and then crumbled beneath its strength.

The light vanished and the creature looked up.

Smiled.

Penny forced her eyes away, strangling a cry.

A door stood ajar seemingly miles ahead and Samantha was

already halfway through it, her back turned. Visions swam before Penny's eyes.

Knocking.

Scratching.

Screaming.

Hands in the dark.

Samantha was going to lock her in.

She was going to die.

Penny sprinted, her injured foot burning.

Something crashed behind her.

She watched Samantha bound out of the room. Watched her turn, pulling the handle as she went.

This was it.

Penny's vision blurred with tears.

She couldn't see where she was going.

Didn't want to see.

She saw the door close in her mind, all light extinguished.

'What are you doing?' Samantha screamed. 'Hurry!'

Penny looked up.

It was still open.

Samantha was still there.

Penny shoved herself through the door and Samantha slammed it shut. Penny stood, panting and exhausted, but Samantha grabbed her arm before she could regain her breath.

'Move,' she hissed, pulling her away from the building.

They ran towards an old church, their feet cracking against the stone and the dog racing alongside them. The day was fading fast, the light only lingering faintly in the sky. Penny could see stars through breaks in the clouds above her.

She could hear something climbing over the metal fence that surrounded the store.

Neither woman said a word. They knew they needed to get inside before the light was gone completely.

Something behind Penny slammed into the ground.

How close was it?

How fast was it?

How much time did they have?

She reached the thick wooden doors of the church, racing past Samantha, who was holding them open and staring directly behind Penny, her eyes wide. As soon as Penny was inside, she slammed them shut, locking them in place with two large beams. The sound reverberated around the room, humming in Penny's head as she sank to her knees, sick and wheezing.

Penny and Samantha sat in silence, eyes closed and chests burning. Even the dog seemed to be out of breath, panting heavily at Samantha's feet. For a short while there was a faint scratching of nails upon wood, but this soon faded and the women were left to the stillness of the church.

Penny swallowed back the memories rushing to the surface of her mind and opened her eyes.

The church was a kaleidoscope of colour. Pinks, yellows and greens swam about the room, coating everything in a rainbow. A large window made of coloured glass filled a wall high above them, and, upon seeing it, Penny began to laugh.

'What is it?' Samantha asked between gasps.

'We're in the brightest room I've ever seen. We're hiding in a room filled with torches.'

Samantha smiled slightly.

'It's bright inside, yes, but the light will fade soon enough. We should be fine as long as we leave quickly once the sun has risen.'

Penny breathed deeply, tasting the colour. The church smelled of smoke and stone, and was deathly still, though not unpleasantly so. It was calming.

Safe.

'Thank you,' Penny said quietly. 'Thank you for not shutting the door.'

Samantha raised an eyebrow.

'You're welcome, but why would I have done that?'

'I don't know.'

Penny lowered her head and stared at the floor, not wanting Samantha to see her blinking back tears. Something heavy pressed against her. She looked up and into the brown eyes of the scraggy dog. It was sitting beside her, leaning into her and staring. Penny scratched it behind the ears.

'Your sister,' she said.

'Rose,' said Samantha.

'Yeah, Rose. You're sure she's with that weird couple?'

'Yes.'

'Those things could have got her. The false ones. On the way or the way back.'

'Yes, but they didn't. I know it.'

'You think they would want to see me? The couple I mean.'

'Like I said, they like… young women. They trust them.'

'Why?'

'I only heard rumours.'

Penny paused, thoughtful. Then she asked, 'How far?'

'Pardon?'

'How far are they? How long would it take?'

'We could be there tomorrow.'

In her mind she saw Mary smile, her face smug as she wrapped an arm around Penny's son. Would she be able to find the river on her own?

Penny sighed.

'Fine. I'll go and look, but if it takes longer than a day I'm gone. I need to go home. Do we have a deal?'

Samantha smiled and held out her hand.

'Deal,' she said.

Penny grabbed the woman's hand and squeezed.

They left the church hours before the sun had risen completely, winding through empty streets still shadowy in the dawn. A brisk wind nibbled at her ears and nose.

There would be a frost soon.

Chapter Ten

'Why don't you tell me about your camp, Penelope? I never knew that there was another safe house nearby. I'd like to hear, if you'd like to tell.'

Penny hissed as she caught her foot in a tree root. By the time she looked up, Samantha was almost entirely out of sight, smothered in brambles and long grass. She stumbled after her.

'Should we be talking? What if we're heard?'

Samantha shrugged and brushed a fly away from her face.

'It's bright enough to keep them still for the time being. Besides, he'll let us know when one is nearby.' She gestured to the dog, who was hopping over fallen branches with ease. Penny glared at him.

'If you say so,' she said.

Samantha turned, allowing Penny to catch up for the moment.

'You won't tell me?'

'There's nothing to tell.'

'Well, how about your family? Your son? What's he like?'

'He's—'

Penny paused.

She tried to picture him, to describe his physical features if nothing else, but her mind couldn't focus on his face.

'He looks like me,' she said, finally.

'And his father?'

'What?'

Samantha smiled, coyly.

'Tell me about his father.'

'He doesn't have one,' Penny snapped. Samantha held up her hands in surrender.

'I apologise, I shouldn't have pushed. Would you tell me about the rest of your family, then?'

Penny clenched her hands into fists.

'Nothing to tell. My mother died scavenging before I could crawl. Apparently night came earlier than their group had planned.

A few people made it back. Said one had got her by the neck and... well, you know. I don't even remember her.'

'And your father?'

A cold hand around her heart.

'Dead.'

'I'm sorry,' said Samantha.

Penny said nothing.

They walked side by side, Samantha slowing her pace to match Penny's limp. Penny pushed herself harder than she should have in order to keep up, sweating beneath her jacket but too proud to ask for a rest. They had been walking non-stop since they left the church and her foot tingled with every step.

'Would you like to hear about Rose?' Samantha asked, holding aside a branch in order for Penny to duck through.

'Whatever you like.'

Samantha laughed.

'You're very sociable, aren't you?'

'And you're amazingly chatty for someone whose sister was kidnapped.'

Penny took immediate pleasure in watching Samantha flinch. The shame came quickly after. She sighed.

'Sorry,' she said. 'Tell me about her. Please.'

She thought maybe she had gone too far, that Samantha had finally seen Penny for who she was and would no longer want to help her find the river even if she did end up managing to find her sister. She opened her mouth to squeeze out another apology, but Samantha spoke first.

'Rose is... naive.'

'Naive?'

'She's only my half-sister. We share a father, but my mother died. Rose was showered in love from the moment she was born, as all children are these days I expect.'

Penny said nothing.

'We kept her from most of the outside, the bad things. Everyone else in the camp loved her. She only knew love and kindness.'

Penny swatted away a fly, rolling her eyes.

'She sounds lovely,' she said. 'But why would that make her naive?'

'I don't think she realises how bad people can be, she has never known them. Even when others in the camp became... too friendly, it was almost as though she couldn't understand their motives.'

'What about the weird couple?'

'They joined our camp late, as I said. They weren't there for very long. We never got a chance to know them before we all left together. I didn't realise they were so... wrong.'

The dog stopped a moment, sniffing at the ground. The women waited for him to finish, then followed him as he bounded off through the trees.

'I don't understand,' Penny said. 'So, all you know about this couple is that they really liked your sister and other people thought they were a bit weird, but you immediately think "kidnapping"? What if Rose is just sitting in their cottage playing cards or something?'

'She's been gone too long for that.'

'What if she liked them more than she liked you?'

Samantha wheeled around, the branch in her hand snapping in two. Her face was flushed.

'Rose loves me. She wouldn't leave me like this. I'm all she has and she's in trouble. We will get her out safely.'

The women glared at each other, neither backing down.

'You know what?' said Penny, scowling. 'I change my—'

A whine echoed through the trees. Samantha broke eye contact, staring around them.

'Where is he?'

Penny turned.

The dog was gone.

They ran through the trees towards the source of the crying, Samantha leaps and bounds ahead of Penny.

'Why the hell can't we just leave it and go? What if those things have it? We could be walking into a trap.'

'How do you think I've been able to survive for this long? That dog finds everything. We need him to get to the cottage and you will need him to get to the river.'

'Shit.'

Another whine, this time close by. Samantha darted to the left and Penny trailed behind, each step harder than the last.

She found them both huddled behind a tall dark shape, covered in moss and ivy. At first glance, it appeared to be two ugly, gnarled trees entwined together in an awful embrace with only a pit of darkness between them. But Penny could see what lay within that darkness. She turned her head, and saw the dog shaking and hiding behind Samantha. Samantha could not tear her eyes away from the shape.

Penny stood frozen to the spot, unable to breathe.

'Get away from it.'

Samantha looked over to Penny, the fear in her eyes showing her true age for the first time since Penny had met her. She could have been no older than Mary. Maybe even the same age as Penny herself.

'Get away from it,' Penny said again, this time through clenched teeth. Her whole body prickled and her foot throbbed like a second heart.

Samantha did not speak, but took a small step back.

And then another.

Something within the tree, hidden in the shadow at its core, seemed to move.

Twitch.

'What is it?' Samantha's voice was barely audible, mostly air. 'A tree?'

'No.'

Penny grimaced. Her eyes followed a thin, branch-like limb, its grey skin so rough and dark it could easily be mistaken for bark. The limb was wrapped around something green and wet. Something that smelled of rot.

The dog whined again, loudly.

Skin peeled away.

A large, wet, dark eye appeared between the moss and darted in the direction of the sound.

Pupils dilated.

Samantha gasped and fell back into the dirt.

Penny remained still.

Calm.

Staring at the long, childlike fingers entwined together inside the grim mass.

'It can't hurt you,' she said quietly. 'Not anymore. It can't move.'

'What is it? What happened to it?'

Slowly the eye began to close.

'Don't you know?' asked Penny quietly. 'This is what happens once they catch you. They grab you, squeeze you, crush you, and then they never let you go. It will stay frozen like this; even after whatever it's holding had rotted away. The forest has grown around this one, but otherwise it's always the same.'

A small breeze danced between the trees, and Penny watched as a matted mass of hair lifted and fluttered in the wind.

'Letting them catch you like this is the only way to stop them.'

The two women walked quickly and silently after that. Penny even complained less. She couldn't afford to stop. To be caught and become... that. She closed her eyes, breathing in the scent of wet leaves and picturing an awful, ugly tree.

A tree with Mary's face on it.

But the face began morphing with another, a man's face, and she tried not to close her eyes after that.

'We'll be there soon. We should probably decide on our plan.'

'Your plan,' said Penny.

Samantha shrugged. 'If you like.'

She sat down on a large tree root and patted the area next to her, smiling at Penny. Penny found Samantha's smile grating on her nerves, like chewing metal. She clenched a fist and sat down beside the other woman, her feet tingling in gratitude for the rest.

Samantha grabbed Penny's hand and looked at her, face calm but stern. Penny resisted the urge to pull away.

'They could be... hostile when you first meet them. You may need to convince them to let you inside. If you mention your son they'll be happy to let you in. I know it.'

Penny began to grow even more uneasy. What on earth had she agreed to? Was it possible she was being led into a trap? The thought had crossed her mind before. She glared at Samantha, who simply waved the look away.

'I know how that sounds, but it's sensible to be suspicious of others around here. They may think you're trying to steal their food. If you mention your son, they will be more trusting of you. They're old souls. They'll believe you to be a good person because you're a mother. Once you're inside, you can't let them know you're looking for Rose, or that you know me.'

'I'm not stupid.'

'Try to find a reason to sneak off. Look around the cottage. There's a cellar; it's where we kept the food. They might be keeping her there.'

'Why would she be in the cellar? You said they liked her. What exactly am I walking into here?'

'You will be safe. They won't hurt you. I'm sure of it.'

'How? Everything you've said so far makes them seem crazy!'

'You will have to trust me.'

Samantha squeezed Penny's hand and Penny pulled it away as if a spider had just crawled over it. Samantha sighed, sadly.

'You don't have to go. I'll understand if you don't. But I won't help you reach the river if you decide not to go through with it. I know that's harsh, but I need my sister back. I would do anything for her.'

'And if I can't find her?'

Samantha looked at the ground.

'I'll still take you to the river. I made a promise, after all.'

Penny rubbed at her hands and stared into the trees. Somewhere, maybe an hour away from where she sat was an eye rolling in its socket, surrounded by leaves.

'I'm not staying long. A few hours at most. I'll go in and search, but then I'm gone. Okay?'

'Yes. Thank you,' said Samantha, relaxing her shoulders. 'That should be more than enough time.'

She stood, and led Penny to a thick bramble bush beside a fallen log, not too far from where they had been sitting.

'I'll wait here for you. If you continue past these trees you'll reach a clearing. Remember to mention your son.'

Penny said nothing and pushed past the bush.

The sooner she started, the sooner she could be on her way home.

Penny slowly crept up to a tree at the edge of the forest and peered around it.

The house at the end of the clearing was small, made of grey brick and surrounded by a ring of sharpened wooden branches. Two figures stood outside, a man and a woman, even older than most of the elders who had resided in the house. They were dressed in tatters, but warmly. They did not seem starved, and the woman was even washing something in a large bowl of water.

They looked completely normal, considering their home was perched on the edge of the forest. But if Samantha said there had been rumours, Penny would be better off being cautious nonetheless.

She peeled herself away from the tree and stepped onto the grass, trying to move slowly but not slow enough to be mistaken for a creature.

They didn't notice her, both carrying on as normal.

Should she make a sound? She didn't want to startle them, but it would be safer than them noticing her only a few feet away.

But what if they just ran and hid?

She needed to get inside the cottage.

Penny sighed and looked down at her foot. She closed her eyes, counted to three and stomped down on the wound, as hard as she could force herself to go.

She shrieked in white-hot agony and fell to the ground in a sweat, panting and shaking.

Confused.

She hadn't expected the pain to be that bad.

Why was it suddenly worse?

Had she damaged it by walking too much?

All thoughts of the couple were washed away by the pain. Penny only recalled her purpose when she looked up and found the man, towering over her. A thick metal pipe inches away from her face.

Penny raised her arms into the air as high as she could manage, twisting her face to make it as scared and exhausted as possible.

This was not all that difficult.

'Who are you?' he said, his face red and blotchy, skin cracked apart by age. 'What do you want? Don't get up, I'll kill you.'

'Please,' Penny said, voice trembling. 'Please, I'm hurt. I don't mean any harm. It hurts. Please, help me.'

'You look fine to me. One more lie and I'll bash your brains in. Who are you? Who told you we were here?'

'No one. No one, I swear. Please, my foot. My foot hurts.'

The man bent over, pipe still aimed at her, and took a quick look at her foot. He winced.

'How the hell did you get here?'

'I don't know! I was separated from my group. I went scavenging. There was an accident and I got separated. I got hurt. I just want to get home. Please help me.'

'If I let you go, you'll kill us for our food. I'm not stupid. Injured or not, you look like you haven't eaten in days. I've seen your type. You'd do anything for what we have.'

'I don't damn well care what you have. I'm hurt and in pain and I just want to get home to my son!'

The main raised the pipe and Penny flinched. When she opened her eyes, she saw that the woman had placed her hand on the man's arm, and was staring intently at Penny.

She hadn't even heard the woman approach them. Her hair was grey and coarse, a mop of wire tied back with a strip of fabric.

'Your son?' she said, as if in a daze. 'You have a son?'

Penny leaned back, almost unconsciously. Something about the woman, the way she stared, wasn't right. Samantha had made them sound peculiar, but this was something else. Perhaps the woman had never met someone able to conceive before.

'Yes,' Penny said, nodding so fast wisps of hair fell into her face. 'He's only five. I need to get back to him. He needs me.'

'I don't understand,' said the woman, her voice was dreamlike, almost childish. 'Women can't conceive. Not anymore. Not since the before times.'

The woman wobbled on her feet and Penny swore she could see tears in her eyes.

'You really have a son? Unaltered?' She paused. 'Human?'

'Yes. Human and little and alone. I need to get home to him. Please help me. Please.'

The woman blinked, wide eyed like a bug.

'Incredible,' the woman whispered.

Penny dug her nails into the skin of her palm.

'Look, I just want to get home. I don't want to cause any trouble. But I'm hurt. I need help. Bandages, water, anything you can spare. I just need a little while and then you'll never have to see me again. Please.'

The pair looked at each other, communicating wordlessly. The woman nodded, very slightly, and then the man looked back at Penny.

'We don't have much,' he said, his voice almost strained, 'but we can offer you some water. Maybe some fabric to bandage yourself.'

The woman stepped forward, eager.

'We have food we can share too. Would you like something to eat? Something to drink?' She nodded at the man, and then to Penny.

'Well, help her up, why don't you?'

He placed his thin arms under her armpits and heaved her to her feet. She stumbled for effect, but stopped short of a whimper. She didn't want to seem too dramatic. Once she seemed to be steady, the man placed a hand on her back and led her towards the house.

Behind her, Penny could have sworn she heard the woman muttering but shrugged it off as her mind playing tricks on her.

'A son,' she thought she had heard her say. 'She has a son.'

Chapter Eleven

The house was clean, free from dust and dirt. The pair had obviously worked hard to make it liveable, covering cracks with weaves of dried flowers. They walked Penny into what appeared to be the living room, a small square space with a large crooked table in its centre. Penny was seated on a thick log topped with a blanket, and given a chipped mug of clean water.

'I'll fetch you something for your foot,' the man said quietly, shuffling out of the room. The door clicked behind him.

Penny sipped the water, staring at the mug to avoid the woman's unblinking stare. A thick black hair floated on the surface.

She winced.

Something above them scraped along the ceiling, slow and purposeful. Penny looked up, catching the woman's gaze. The woman smiled, hiding her teeth behind full, cracked lips. She did not look away, and she did not offer an explanation for the noise. Goosebumps prickled at Penny's skin.

It was with relief that she turned to face the man, who had just re-entered the room. He was carrying an old shirt, ragged but clean looking, and a large bowl of water.

'This is all we have,' the man said, holding out the shirt. 'Sorry.'

Penny forced a smile and reached out to take it but the woman was there first, moving at a speed Penny never would have suspected for someone of her age. The woman glared at the man, shirt held to her chest.

'Don't be rude, Harry,' she said, voice trembling and quiet. 'She's injured. You need to help her.'

The man blinked, nodded, and kneeled in front of Penny. She flushed.

'You don't have to do that, really.'

The older woman's head snapped towards her. She smiled.

'We insist.'

The man removed Penny's sandal and placed her foot into the bowl of cold water. With gentle fingers the man brushed against her foot, pulling away the old bandage and washing the dirt around the wound. Penny hissed as his long fingernails scraped across her skin, and she looked away when she saw the water start to turn brown.

The woman was again sitting in front of Penny, staring and smiling.

'I'm sorry about before,' she said. 'You're the first person we've seen since we left our group. You gave us quite a scare. My name is Olivia, and this is Harry. It's a pleasure to meet you.'

'Likewise,' said Penny, smiling awkwardly. The three of them sat in an uncomfortable silence. Olivia coughed.

'And?' she said.

'Sorry?'

'What is your name?'

'Oh. Penelope. It's Penelope.'

Penny could hear her heartbeat in her ears. It was too quiet. Nobody was speaking, and so she began to speak aloud if only to cover up the sound of silence. She said her words slowly; careful not to slip in any information she should not have known.

'You said you left your group,' she said. 'Why? I mean, surely it would have been safer being all together.'

'They were not good people,' Olivia replied, a little too quickly to be casual. 'They were dangerous.'

Harry began tearing the shirt into long strips. Penny watched him put several of these to one side, and then begin to dry her foot with what was left of the shirt. Once she was dry, he wrapped the strips around the wound.

'Dangerous how?'

A stray strand of hair fell onto Olivia's face. She grabbed it instantly and poked it back into place. Her nails were yellow and long, with something crusted beneath them.

'We had different views, different ideas on how to live, and they didn't like that, I presume. We didn't feel welcome, or safe. In the end, it was easier to leave and live the way we wanted. Even if that meant living alone.'

'Isn't it hard? Being here by yourself?'

'Yes, sometimes, but we get by. Tell us about yourself, Penelope. Your son. You said you had a son.'

'Uh, yes, I do. I'm from a large group of people in the hills. And we—'

'How old is he?'

'Sorry?'

'Your son. How old is he?'

'He's five.'

Olivia leaned forward on her stool as Harry finished up and sat beside her. The strand fell back onto her face, but this time she did not adjust it.

'And he's healthy? He must be. You look very strong. Strong blood creates strong children. You didn't tell me his name. What is his name?'

A strange pressure filled the room, seeping into Penny's head and against her chest. This wasn't right. It wasn't right at all. She'd felt safer in the forest. Why had she agreed to this? She should have found the damn river by herself.

Still, she had made an agreement, hadn't she?

Penny brought the mug to her lips, and then allowed it to fall from her hand. The mug hit the ground and rolled, water spilling and pooling on the floor like blood.

'Oh God. I'm really sorry,' Penny said, her voice wavering. 'I just... I'm just tired. And my foot hurts. I'm so clumsy.'

Olivia and Harry were still for a moment and Penny was starting to worry that she had been a little too over dramatic. Olivia began whispering into Harry's ear. He nodded once, and turned back to his guest.

'If you'd like to stay for the night,' he said, 'we have food that we would be willing to share with you. And a spare bed. It's not much, but it's warmer than outside. Then you could carry on your journey tomorrow when you're properly rested.'

'You really should rest,' Olivia added, staring at her almost hungrily now. 'You need your strength.'

'Thank you,' said Penny, 'but I really can't stay too long. Would it be rude of me to ask if I could rest for just a few hours? I'd love to take a nap if I could. Somewhere dry.'

She laughed nervously. Olivia leaned closer.

'Surely there's no rush?' she said, a little hastily now. 'You'll get further if you've rested properly. You'll stay the night and I won't hear any more about it. Harry, help her up.'

'Oh no, thank you but I can't. I really need to get back to my son as soon as I can.'

'That's... a shame,' said Olivia. 'But if you're sure. Harry will help you to the spare room. Feel free to sleep for as long as you like. You are more than welcome to stay.'

Penny started to thank Olivia, but Harry had already hoisted her to her feet, and she was being pushed firmly out of the room. He led her through a narrow corridor and up an even narrower flight of stairs. The pair of them could barely fit at the same time, and Penny's arm grazed across the stone wall as she moved.

All the windows on the second floor had been boarded up, thick planks of wood blocking every trace of the outside. Handmade shelves lined the walls, candles and drooping plants filling every inch of them.

'How did you get hold of this many candles?' Penny asked, awestruck. 'Is it safe to have so many?'

Harry shrugged.

'Made some. Took others. Boards keep the light in.'

'Uh... right.'

He stopped outside one of several closed doors, pulled a small metal key from his pocket, and inserted it into the lock. A deep metallic clunk came from within, and the door swung open.

Penny hesitated.

'Do you lock all your doors?'

'Usually. It's safer. In case something gets in during the night.'

'That happens often?'

'Not yet. Better to be safe.'

Penny grimaced. Harry guided her into the room and she limped inside, feeling the presence of the door, and the heavy, metal lock. She sank down onto a wooden bed frame lined with blankets and dried leaves.

'Thank you,' she said to Harry, as he began to leave her. 'I really won't be long. It's really nice of you to let me rest.'

'Stay as long as you like,' the man grumbled. He pulled open the door and went to shut it behind him.

'If you wouldn't mind,' Penny said quickly in a voice that sounded almost desperate, 'could you leave the door open? I'm just more comfortable that way.'

Harry shrugged, and retreated out of the room.

Penny slowly fell onto her side, lying on top of the itchy woollen blankets and watching as Harry pulled the door half-closed. She shut her eyes, and then listened very carefully.

Ten long seconds passed before she heard footsteps move away from the door and recede down the corridor. She waited until the sound had faded completely, and then pushed herself up off the bed.

She crept to the door and peered around it into the hall.

It was deserted.

She stepped out.

There were two other doors in the corridor, each one shut. Calling out to Rose would be stupid, not least because she was convinced the young woman was already dead. Penny would have to try every door, and hope that the weird couple stayed downstairs.

Penny opened the door closest to her. It opened easily and without creaking.

Nothing.

A bedroom, an almost identical replica of the room she had come from, if a little larger. Nowhere for a young woman to hide. Penny cast a quick, curious glance at an old photograph on the bedside table, in which a young woman was smiling proudly in a large white coat, then closed the door and moved on.

The second door was at the end of the corridor, probably the bathroom. Penny grabbed the handle and pushed lightly.

The door did not budge.

She pushed again, twisting at the handle.

Nothing.

The door was locked.

Why bother to lock a bathroom door?

She breathed in for courage and rapped at the door with her knuckles.

'Rose?' she said, just a whisper. A loud thump and the scraping of wood was her reply.

There was a sound below her feet.

Movement.

Footsteps.

They were coming.

There was nowhere to hide.

Without thinking, Penny ran into the larger of the bedrooms, pushing the door shut behind her. She crouched, eye pressed up against the keyhole.

Through the dust and spider webs, Penny saw Olivia run past the door with Harry at her heels. She was heading to the locked room.

Muffled behind the door, but still perfectly legible, Penny heard her speak.

'For goodness sake, Harry. Hurry up and fix that door while I check on her.'

Her.

So Rose was actually here. Penny would have to remember to apologise to Samantha, once she escaped from this place.

A dark shadow that must have been Harry moved in front of the keyhole, blocking her view. There was a muffled, but audible, clunk.

Harry stepped away from the keyhole.

The door opposite, the door she was meant to be safely sleeping behind, was shut.

Locked.

Rose was no longer important.

Penny needed to get out.

Now.

Somewhere beyond her vision, a door closed.

Somebody, something, screamed.

'How is she?' Harry asked, 'What happened? Is she hurt?'

'She's fine. Just agitated, poor thing. We need to get started as soon as possible, Harry. I can't bear seeing her like this, not when we're this close.'

Olivia sniffed.

'It will be okay. It will be okay. We can start tonight now, can't we?'

Another sniff, and then a mumble Penny couldn't quite make out.

A shadow moved past the keyhole once more, and then down the stairs. Penny swallowed, head pounding.

Guilt gnawed at her, an uncomfortable thought at the back of her head. They were planning something, something to do with her and Rose.

Penny had done many questionable things in her life, but only to people who had deserved it. Did Rose really deserve to be abandoned in this house?

Penny bit her lip, already aware of the answer. Still, what could she do? The door was locked. Did Samantha expect her to beat the old couple and then smash the door down? It would be safer to escape and find Samantha first. Penny could let her know Rose was inside, and then let her do all the dirty work.

Her mind was made up.

Carefully she pushed open the door and edged her way out of the room. She scanned the corridor, checking for movement.

Her gaze fell upon an open door, a crack of light spilling out into the hall.

They had left the bathroom door open.

Penny looked over her shoulder, towards the way out, and then back at the open door. She cried out.

Olivia was standing in the open doorway.

She was not smiling.

Strong hands grabbed Penny from behind. She thrashed and screamed, kicking out at anything she could. Something was pushed into her mouth, soft and stale, and something else covered her eyes. Her arms were brought close together behind her back, bound tight.

She was dragged, mute and blind, down the stairs, through a door, and then down more stairs. She dug in her heels, shrieking louder with the pain but not loud enough for anyone to hear.

Who was there to hear her, anyway?

Cool air hit her skin, and the light that she could see through her blindfold went dark.

She was shoved roughly against a stone wall and Penny slammed against it, feeling the arms release her. She pushed away from the wall, running in any direction she could, but her foot caught on something long and thin and she tumbled to the floor, face first.

She could taste blood.

Her legs were pushed together and wrapped with rope.

Footsteps and then, in the distance, a faint click.

Penny could hear a door close, far away.

Nearby.

The energy in her body evaporated, and she screamed in frustration until her voice grew hoarse.

Only echoes replied.

Before #4

The room was suffocatingly hot and stuffy, the warmest summer Penny could remember since she had been very small and her father had still been with her. Of course, the largeness of her stomach did nothing to help matters.

Her swollen belly was tight against her thin dress, and Penny rested a hand gently upon it. Her other hand shot up to her cheek to wipe away a tear.

'I'm sorry,' she said, voice trembling. 'It's... it's just very hard to talk about.'

Someone coughed awkwardly, and Penny looked up with red, sore eyes. The elders, eight of them since the eldest died last month, were all sitting at a table in front of her. The two women stared at her sadly, one casually trying to wipe away a tear of her own. Most of the men stared anywhere but at Penny, some of them very red faced. The man in the centre of their group, his face sunken and grey, scratched at his chin without looking her in the eyes.

'Just explain it as best you can, Penelope. Tell us the truth.'

Penny sniffed and nodded slightly, again rubbing her stomach.

'It... was around February. Sometime around then, I don't remember exactly.'

'That's okay. Just tell us as best you can.'

Penny looked down.

'We'd been getting along. Becoming friends. He'd... been having a hard time with Mary and I was trying to cheer him up. I thought we were friends but he... he...'

'Do we have to make her do this?' whispered one of the women. The man in the centre nodded.

'It's only fair. Go on, Penelope.'

She took a shuddering breath, and then exhaled.

'He... must have thought I liked him. I must have given him the wrong impression. I went to cheer him up and he shut the door. He pushed me down and... and he pulled up my dress.'

Her voice broke and she began to sob, tears falling onto fists now clenched in her lap. She took a moment to control herself, to catch her breath, and then continued.

'He told me no one would believe me. He said everyone whispered about me, about my lies, and that everyone knew he had Mary. He said people wouldn't believe me. So I didn't say anything. And then...'

She stroked her stomach, smiled through the tears.

'When I started getting bigger, I knew everyone would believe me. They had to.'

The elder sighed and rubbed his temples.

'Penelope, nobody can deny that you are pregnant.'

'That remains to be seen,' countered a short man with a large beard. 'She could just be gaining weight. A false pregnancy isn't out of the question either. There hasn't been a real pregnancy here in twenty-seven years, and unless you've been working on the infertility crisis without telling us, the odds are very much against her. Besides, we don't even know *what* she'll give birth to.'

The first elder scratched at his face.

'That's mostly true,' he said. 'I'm not discounting that. Though it's highly unlikely the child would be anything but human. Her parents had both been too young to receive the treatment, after all.' He paused, and then nodded to himself. 'Yes, I think for the moment we have to assume that she is pregnant with a human child, and so, we have to determine who the father is and... how it came about.'

'Sir?' said Penny.

All eyes fell on her once more.

'Yes, Penelope?'

'You don't understand.' Her voice cracked. 'He doesn't deny what happened.'

'I beg your pardon?'

Penny's lip began to tremble.

'He's proud.'

Penny was asked to return to her room before Lewis was brought in, but she told them she wanted to stay nearby.

'I'd feel safer near you,' she whispered, gripping an elder

woman's hand tightly. 'Please don't make me be alone. Not right now.'

The elders agreed to her request, and Penny was made as comfortable as possible in the adjoining room. Once they had left her, Penny rose and waddled over to the door, pulling it open just enough to hear the proceedings. She dragged over a chair, sat and listened.

The door in the next room creaked, and then closed. There was a quiet scraping as a chair was pulled across the floor.

'Lewis,' came the voice of the main elder after a moment of silence. 'Do you know why you're here?'

'It's that lying little bitch,' shrieked Mary. 'That little whore!'

'Remove her, please.'

'I am not leaving.'

'Then for goodness sake be quiet.' When no argument was made, the elder continued. 'Lewis? Can you tell me why you're here?'

'No, sir. No, I don't know why I'm here.'

'We are investigating Penelope's pregnancy. There have been some rumours. Can you tell me what you know?'

'What has the bitch told you? What did she say? It's all her fault this happened, she seduced him!'

'Hush, Mary. They don't need to know all that.'

'Lewis,' said the elder. 'I'm going to be blunt, and I need you to answer me honestly. Are you the father of Penelope's child?'

'Oh yes. Yes, I am. What I did was awful, really, but it didn't cause any real lasting damage and I won't do it again. I'm sure we'll all be able to get along. Won't we?'

Penny could hear the smile in his voice. She closed her eyes and could instantly see the dopey grin he would have on his face. Eyes blank and uncomprehending. There was a long silence in the room. Eventually one of the elders said quietly, 'Thank you, Lewis. That will be all for now.'

Penny closed the door, and moved back to her original place in the room, dragging the chair behind her. When the elders re-entered, she was humming to her stomach. They waited in the doorway until she pretended to notice them. Her eyes grew wide.

'What happened?' she asked. One of the women pushed past the other elders, walked over to Penny and held her very gently.

'You poor thing,' she mumbled. 'Don't worry. We'll sort this for you. You'll be safe now.'

Penny, with some effort, put her arms around the woman and hugged her back.

She smiled.

Chapter Twelve

It was the dripping that woke her.

Close by and loud enough to echo around her aching head each time another droplet fell.

Penny groaned and her dry tongue brushed up against coarse fabric like sandpaper against stone. For a moment, still groggy with sleep, she panicked.

She tried to remove the foreign object from her mouth but couldn't.

She couldn't breathe.

She was suffocating.

She cried out but the sound was muffled.

Stop, said a voice. *Calm down. Relax. Breathe.*

Think.

She was in a cottage and she was looking for someone. Samantha. No, Rose. She was looking for Rose. Rose was behind a door but the door was locked and everything went black and the scraping and...

Damn it, breathe.

The old couple. They had caught her. Tied her up and left her here. She must have fallen asleep or collapsed from the fatigue. But for how long? She couldn't see anything with the blindfold.

Then let's deal with that first, she thought, pushing herself from her sitting position onto her side. Her face hit stone and her head throbbed in reply. Penny bit down on the fabric in her mouth until the pain faded and she could think again.

She took a breath, readying herself for the pain, and then began to scrape her face along the floor.

It hurt a little, but not nearly as much as she was expecting. Penny rubbed her face against the stone as hard as she could, moving until the fabric around her eyes became loose and eventually fell away. She sat back up and shook her head, flinging the fabric across the room. She blinked a few times and squinted.

There was not much of an improvement. The room was still

pitch black, a darkness almost impossible to penetrate. Almost. Penny could just about make out outlines of certain aspects of the room – a bowl, a wooden staircase and beyond that, the outline of a closed door.

She shuddered and ignored the rising panic, then locked her eyes on the bowl. Goal in sight, she collapsed onto the floor once more, this time focusing on her gag. It came off almost immediately, and Penny drank in the air, gasping and spluttering.

Against the cool air, the dryness of her mouth was even more pronounced – an autumn leaf shrunken and shrivelled. She had to peel her tongue away from the roof of her mouth and it came away with a crack. Penny turned to the bowl and, she realised, the sound of the dripping.

Still bound at her hands and feet, Penny was forced to crawl towards the noise. Her mouth filled with saliva as the dripping grew louder. Her forehead hit plastic and something in front of her toppled and fell. Cool water pooled around her and Penny almost shrieked in despair. She scrambled forward, hoping to save some of the water but there was no time. With burning cheeks, she began sipping at the puddle on the floor around her.

It was not enough, but it would have to do.

Hair dripping, Penny turned to the staircase. Her nails, brittle and snapped, dug into the stone.

There would be plenty of water upstairs.

As Penny pulled at the ropes, she thought about Mary. Whether it was the dark, locked room or her still groggy head, she wasn't sure, but her thoughts drifted again and again to the woman's thin, plain face.

What would Penny's life have been like had Mary not been such a coward? At the very least she wouldn't be here right now. Penny would probably be in her room, next to her father, listening to him talk about the old days. She had loved his stories of large cities full of people, full of children like her. He told her tales of evenings where men and women could walk hand in hand beneath the stars, and how his own parents had met each other beside an ocean – something Penny would never see.

Penny could have spent her whole life listening to her father's stories, if not for Mary.

She had heard what Mary said about her, of course. Mary liked to think of *her* as the coward. A liar or a whore, depending on the day.

'She'll never admit to what she's done,' Penny had heard her say one evening, a group of women half listening as Mary ranted.

'She's ruined my life, and she'll never admit it.'

Penny had scoffed then. She knew Mary would never do anything to her directly. She thought there was nothing to worry about.

That had been a mistake, she supposed. She should have realised a woman capable of ruining her life once would try it again.

Penny grunted and twisted her wrists painfully. The ropes moved slightly, but not enough. She wouldn't be able to pull herself loose like this. She might have been able to cut the rope on something, but without being able to see the room properly there was little chance of that.

She took a deep breath.

All she really needed was a hand loose. One hand would make everything else much simpler, so start with that.

She bit her lip and began to move her wrists again.

She wriggled them up and down, pulling with one wrist to force the rope to tighten around it, and so enable more space around the other. Sweat trickled down her neck. The rope was growing loose. She had just started to pull one hand free when a beam of light pushed into the darkness.

Penny immediately stopped what she was doing and desperately tried not to panic. Her head ran through lists of possible ways to escape the situation but nothing would help and she knew it. If they came closer, they would see she was no longer blindfolded and then she would be back to square one, if they didn't deal with her right then. She curled into herself on the ground, covering her face with her knees and tried to control her breathing.

The footsteps grew louder, in time with the beating of her heart, but came to a halt halfway down the staircase.

'Harry, what are you doing?'

'I thought I'd give her some water. We don't want her to die down here. She looked really sick before.'

'And what if you'd woken her up?'

'Sorry, Olivia.'

A sigh.

'It doesn't matter,' Olivia said. 'I don't care. She has a son, Harry. This is more than we could ever have hoped for. It will work this time. We're so close.'

'I know, I know. I still think it would be better if she was healthy, though. Couldn't we wait a little longer, for her to get better first?'

'And what if she doesn't get better? What if she dies while we wait? We'll never get a chance like this again, Harry. Never. We've already lost Rose.'

'It was the least we could do for Samantha, you know that.'

Penny's heart sank, a stone in an icy lake.

'I don't trust her, Harry. She lied about bringing us the woman, to take back her sister. I don't like it. I wanted them both.'

'But we have the best one. The woman. That's all that matters. You said so.'

'I suppose,' said Olivia. 'I'll just feel better when this is all over and everything is right again. When everything is how it should have been from the very start.'

Penny did not hear the rest. She was numb, and far away. In a log house, surrounded in white.

Samantha had set her up. Had left her here to die.

She had been abandoned again.

Why did everyone hate her so much? What had she done to deserve being abandoned and betrayed, over and over?

This was all Mary's fault.

All Penny had ever wanted was to be near her family, first her father and later, her son. Safe and happy. Mary had taken all that away.

Isolated and abandoned her in this forest.

It was Mary's fault she had become pregnant.

It was Mary's fault her son no longer had his mother with him.

It was Mary's fault these people now wanted to lock her away in the dark.

Penny's world spiralled, a chaotic cyclone with Mary at its centre. A door slammed.

Get up.

Penny pulled one hand free from its bindings, followed by the other. The rope fell softly to the ground.

Brush off.

Penny stretched her hands, rolling them at the wrist joint. They were tender, probably bruised, but free.

Now for her ankles.

Move on.

She pulled her feet towards her, as close as she could get them and began to blindly run her hands along the rope, searching for knots or weak points. She started to pull with her ankles, hoping to untie them in a similar way to how she had released her wrists. She tugged then bit down on her tongue to suppress a scream.

As she pulled, the rope tightened against her injured foot and something burst. There was a sickening pressure, followed by warm, oozing liquid running down her foot onto the floor. Vomit threatened to crawl up her throat, but the last thing Penny wanted was to be tied up, leaking and covered in sick. She swallowed it down as the tears began to fall.

She twisted her pulsing foot to free the other. The rope scraped across it. Agony.

She breathed deep, shuddered, and tried again, this time pulling with her other foot. The rope began to tighten around it, as it had with her wrists. There was now just enough space to wriggle out of the rope. The only problem was she would need to use the injured foot. The thought made her queasy, but there was no time to do anything else. Penny bunched up her vest, stuffing the fabric between her teeth and biting down. Then, she began to pull her foot through the rope.

When she had given birth to her son, the elders told her how lucky she was. How she would never have to go through anything as painful as that again.

The elders had been wrong.

Her entire body clenched and trembled as the rope squeezed over her swollen ankle and towards her wound.

She wailed against the fabric in her teeth, hands twitching. Her head rolled and her hair clung to her forehead, dripped in sweat.

She wanted to peel off her skin. To cut off her foot, anything to stop the pain.

She did not stop.

One more push, she thought as liquid seeped down across her foot.

One more push, she thought as the room swam.

Just one.

More.

Push.

She pushed.

Her foot came free and the pressure stopped. Lights flashed in her vision, and Penny managed to twist away just in time to vomit.

Panting, angry, she kicked the rope off her other foot and stood. Her foot screamed and she ignored it, limping towards the wooden staircase.

At the top was the door, outlined in weak grey light.

Ajar.

Penny enveloped herself in her black thoughts as she climbed the stairs, leaving nothing but darkness.

Though there had been light when the door was opened into what she now knew as a basement, Penny was surprised to find that the sun had already set. Grim moonlight filled the hallway she was standing in, making the room fuzzy and difficult to see.

She closed the door behind her without making a noise and melted into the shadows. A strand of hair tickled against her nose as she breathed deeply.

Calmly.

The house was silent and cold. An icy breeze caressed her arms as Penny stood and tried to recall where the entrance was. She winced, and then slowly ran her fingers across her bare shoulders. They had taken her jacket.

'Damn it,' she hissed, pushing back her knotted hair.

Going back outside, especially in the dead of night, was already dangerous enough. Without clothing, she was as good as dead.

Unless she borrowed some.

Penny leaned against the wall behind her and sighed as deeply as she could without making a sound. She counted to three, and then peeled herself away, edging towards the door at the end of the room and leaving it ajar behind her.

She scanned the shadows, searching for anything that would give her a clue to where she was, but only seeing grey. The breeze came again, tickling her ears. She followed it through the dark and through another open door then smiled to herself.

The breeze had led her to the hallway. The front door was there, right in front, calling to her. Penny wanted nothing more than to listen to the voice screaming in her head, open it and run far away from Olivia, Harry, Samantha and all of them. But it was the stairs she needed, just opposite the door. The stairs that would lead her further into the house.

Penny bit her lip, ripping off chapped skin with her teeth, as she slowly began to climb the stairs.

The second floor was uncomfortably silent, like a predator not wanting to be noticed. Three doors. Two bedrooms, one unknown. Unlocked, now that Rose was probably gone.

A monstrous wave of anger rose inside of her. She let it.

To her left was the smaller of the two bedrooms, the one she had originally been led to. Penny pressed herself against the door and listened for movement. Satisfied with the silence, she opened the door and slipped inside.

She grabbed the stiff woollen blankets still strewn across the bed and wrapped them around her torso. There was nothing else in the room, and Penny had just decided to risk the outside as she was when she heard a noise.

A murmur.

Voices.

The words were unclear, but they were definitely voices. Penny was dizzy with fear and rage. She wanted to run, to hurt them, to scream, to cry, to shout, everything at once. She trembled and stumbled to the door, and then out into the hallway.

She stared in front of her at the darkness, unblinking and straining to hear. The murmurs were coming from the bedroom opposite her. It would be easy to burst in and take the couple by surprise. To make them pay for everything. On the other hand, there was still time to leave. Penny could creep down the stairs now and never have to see these people again. She could find the river. Find her way home to her son. To Mary.

The name caused her anger to flash, white hot.

Would this be what would happen when she saw Mary again? Would she be too frightened to take revenge? Too weak? Too cowardly?

Penny needed to take control.

She reached for the handle, only to stop short as the murmurs grew louder. Closer.

Mind blank with panic, Penny found herself turning and running down the hallway, cursing both her cowardice and her stupidity. She had turned the wrong way. Away from the staircase. The voices were already louder – it would be too late to turn back and head into the other bedroom now. There was only one place to hide.

She stumbled into the only other room in the hall, eyes closed.

She was sure that the strange couple would be close behind her and she couldn't bear to look. She pushed the door shut with her back and opened her eyes as she gasped for air.

She winced and only just managed to stop herself crying out with pain.

The room was filled with orange light, an inferno that burned her eyes. Tears streamed down her face, but Penny couldn't look away.

There was something within the light, through the blur of her tears. She blinked, momentarily bringing the room into view. A bathroom, tiled, and almost every surface covered with candles. An army of flames.

A silhouette among them.

What was that?

She blinked again.

The silhouette grew clearer, its edges sharp.

There was something in the bath. Something small and pale beneath the shimmering water.

Something seemingly not breathing.

Something with a wide, white smile.

Chapter Thirteen

Penny found herself frozen, not even able to blink. Every hair on her body prickled, a static shiver that rolled across her in a wave.

Light glittered across the still bathwater, casting dancing shadows across the pale face of the creature below.

Death lay smiling before her.

A choked cry escaped from her throat, soon followed by burning tears. Penny forced her eyes closed, shivering and waiting for the end.

Nothing happened.

As the seconds dragged on, almost in slow motion, her breathing began to slow. Cautiously, she opened her eyes.

The creature had not moved. It lay as it had before, encased in water. Surrounded by candles and a cloud of long, dark hair.

Candles.

Light.

Of course.

The room was so bright even Penny felt disorientated. To one of those things…

Penny lifted her foot gently away from the tiled floor and stepped closer to the creature. Her chest burned and her temples throbbed as she realised she had stopped breathing.

She couldn't breathe.

Not yet.

Closer.

Just a bit closer.

Penny paused beside the flames and stared down into the water, careful not to move her head into the creature's line of sight. Just in case.

Nothing. No movement at all.

As if pulled by invisible wires, Penny watched her hand rise and edge towards the water. The shadow of her fingers scuttled across the surface.

She regained her control a hair's breadth from the creature's face. Its eyes were open, staring but unseeing. Pools of void.

She had never seen one this close. Nobody had.

It was so like a child, so like her son, she could almost imagine feeling for the creature. Its long arms floated lifelessly in the water, dark tapered fingers like daggers. Entwined with the creature's fingers was a long plastic tube. It seemed to start in the wrist and ended in a coiled pile on the floor. The end was crusted with blood.

Penny frowned and stared back into the creature's face.

It wasn't right.

Where the skin should have been grey, it was instead an ashy pink. There was even a hint of blood in the false child's face.

Penny's hand, still hovering over the creature, twitched.

A small bubble of air escaped from its open mouth. Its chest rose and fell.

Penny snatched her hand away and held it close, stumbling backward. Her heart was pounding in her ears, threatening to slam its way out of her rib cage.

Was it breathing?

How was it breathing?

They couldn't breathe.

They were dead.

They had always been dead.

Had it seen her through the light?

It couldn't.

It wasn't possible.

How much time did she have?

She backed up to the bathroom door, her gaze locked onto the bath, but the creature did not stir.

It was alive. Breathing. It shouldn't be able to breathe. That was not how they were. Was this one different?

How could this happen?

Wait.

Calm.

If it could breathe...

Penny pulled at the blanket wrapped around her until a long strip had been torn away. She rolled it into a ball the size of her fist, and slowly approached the bath. The creature did not move. Not even when Penny pushed the fabric into its mouth, clamping her other hand around its small nose.

The creature trembled once, and then lay still.

Penny would take control, one person, and one monster, at a time.

Olivia was staring out of a grimy window, one hand delicately lifting the corner of the cardboard that covered it. Harry was on all fours behind her, scrubbing at the floorboards, with his metal pipe propped carelessly against the wall beside him.

The door to the bedroom had been opened by the time Penny crept over to it, the first lucky break she had experienced for some time. From her position in the hallway, she watched as Harry finished his scrubbing and then turned to Olivia.

'It's done. We can start soon if you want.'

'Do you think it's going to be stormy?' Olivia asked, not looking behind her and therefore unable to notice Penny quietly grab the pipe as she entered the room.

'No idea. Maybe. Why?'

'I just like the thought of it. I think a lightning storm would be fitting.'

'Well, I can go get the woman, but I can't do anything about the—'

Penny swung the pipe against Harry's head, hard.

He stumbled, but did not fall.

She hit him again and again.

Olivia turned and began to scream, running over as Harry fell to the ground. Penny held out the pipe towards her, smiling grimly, her face speckled with blood.

'Hello, Olivia,' she said. 'I think we have a few things we need to talk about.'

'Please,' Olivia moaned, face growing white and eyes growing wide. Penny hated those eyes. They reminded her of Mary's.

'Please. Please don't hurt me. Oh, Harry. What have you done?'

'Nothing you weren't going to do to me, I'm sure.'

Olivia rose to her feet and backed up until she was pressed against the wall. Penny did not move, keeping her good foot on Harry while she pointed the pipe towards the woman. Her hands were red and dripping onto the floor.

'Well? You want to tell me what you had in store for me?'

Olivia shook her head.

Penny slammed the pipe into the wall. It clanged loudly, and Olivia flinched.

'Nothing,' she said. 'We weren't going to do anything. I swear.'

'I'll tell you what, the less you lie to me the less I'll hit you. I am in a very bad mood, so I really wouldn't push it if I were you.'

Olivia swallowed, then for a moment seemed to gather her courage.

She stepped forward and raised her head, staring directly into Penny's eyes.

'I'm trying to help you. Help everyone.'

Penny laughed.

Olivia scowled at her.

'Mock me if you like, but I know more about the children than you ever will. I was there when birth rates plummeted and the 'treatment' was announced. Men and women cried with joy as they lined the streets, waiting for their turn to be inseminated. I watched with the world as the new children were born, and ten years later I mourned when every last one of them died.'

She leaned forward, hissing the words.

'I saw them rise, grey skinned and dark eyed from the dirt. I hid as the world crumbled like a house of cards. It was quick. We never had a chance. Not then. But I know them now. I can fix them.'

Penny pointed the pipe at her again.

'I don't care what you lived through. I don't care what you saw. What were you going to do to *me*?'

Penny watched Olivia's eyes dart around the room, looking for an escape, before settling back onto her face.

'We needed someone like you.'

'Someone like me?'

'A woman. A young woman.'

CHAPTER THIRTEEN

Olivia reached out a hand to Penny, and took another step forward.

'We couldn't stand being in that group. Me and Harry, we wanted something more. It was unbearable, being stuck in that house and following their rules when I knew I could fix it. Fix everything. Those poor children, out in the woods, all alone.'

She clenched her bony hands into two tight knots, and pressed them into her stomach.

'I... We couldn't bear it anymore. We left. We planned to set up a small home in the forest for us, and for the children. We wanted Rose to stay. She almost did, until her nosey sister got suspicious and took her away. Rose was going to help us.'

Penny's hand creaked against the metal pipe as it involuntarily tightened.

'Help you? You locked her in a room with that... thing.'

'Shut your mouth,' Olivia snapped. 'Don't you talk about her like that.'

'Her? It's not a "her". It's not human and it never has been, no matter what you think you saw.'

Penny watched as a single tear rolled down Olivia's cheek.

'She was, once, and she will be again. Soon. I told you, I know how to fix them.'

She smiled, her teeth the colour of a winter's sky, and took another step forward. It was as though she was challenging Penny to stop her.

Penny said nothing. She stood motionless. Beside her the one solitary candle of the room began to flicker in the evening breeze.

'I made another little girl first, but she wasn't perfect. Wasn't right, not for us. I gave her to someone who needed her. A friend. I just got the measurements wrong. I thought it would only take a little, just now and then, but that won't work. Not forever. I know what to do now.'

She licked her lips.

'You must understand. It wasn't necessarily Rose we needed. She was just the youngest of the house. Samantha was too old, as was I. But you...'

She smiled again, dreamily.

'You have already produced a natural child. You turned up on our doorstep like a gift from God. You're exactly what we... What I... need.'

Penny laughed again, a sound closer to a bark coming from her dry throat.

'And how exactly was I going to help you "fix" them? Or was that not it at all? Maybe you were going to make me pregnant, rape me and steal the child.' She gestured to Harry with her free hand, still crumpled on the ground. 'I really don't think he'll be up to that for a while, do you?'

Olivia frowned.

'Heavens no. That would be barbaric.'

With a frail hand, she reached up and stroked Penny's cheek. Her eyes grew wide and glassy as she stared at Penny like she had in the living room. Hungrily. Sweat scratched Penny's skin as she slapped the old woman's hand away.

Olivia continued to smile.

'I told you. I was there when it all started. I saw them. I *know* them. They're just babies. Children. They can't help what they are. What happened to them. But I can change them. Transform them back into what they had been. Into children again. All it takes is the right person.' Olivia lashed out, scratching her nails across Penny's cheek. 'And a little blood.'

Neither woman moved.

The candle flickered in the breeze once more as blood mingled with the sweat on Penny's face.

'Oh, I can give you blood,' she said, and raised the pipe high.

Olivia smiled again.

'It won't matter. She'll be awake soon no matter what you do.'

Penny smiled back.

'Fuck you,' she said, and swung the pipe down across the old woman's skull.

Night had fallen by the time Penny had finished in the house. There was nowhere to go until the shadows released her, no safety outside, so even now she was trapped within. She had gained nothing, at least until sunrise.

Penny huddled against a stone wall and stared up to the ceiling. To where she thought the bathroom would be. Somewhere above her, the warped image of a child floated dead in a bath of water. At least, she hoped it was dead. Penny stared and stared, forgetting to blink until stinging tears forced their way out of her eyes.

How could she ever be completely sure it was dead when it had looked lifeless to begin with?

What if it was climbing out of the bath now, trailing water as is dragged itself down the hallway?

Towards the stairs.

Towards her.

A cool wind brushed up against her skin, and her mind buzzed with sleep deprivation.

Had Olivia been right? Had she known a way of changing the creatures? What if Penny had destroyed humanity's first real chance at taking back their world?

Or was Olivia just a sick old woman?

A very lucky, sick old woman.

Penny looked up again and shuddered.

Eventually the paranoia faded, only to be replaced with the sickening thrum of pain that shot out in waves from her foot. A throbbing that matched her heartbeat. Penny let the pulsing roll through her body, relaxing into the rhythm of her blood.

She did not realise she had slept until several minutes after waking, her eyes heavy, her stomach empty and her mouth dry.

She dragged herself from her slumped position on the hard, wood floor up onto her knees. Her body was tight and stiff, as if shrunken from being left out in the rain for too long. Penny stretched her arms slowly, but the pain did not ease. She sighed, grabbed her metal pipe, and used it to push herself up onto her good foot before allowing the injured one to touch the ground.

Carefully, Penny hobbled over to the front door. Faint light spilled out from beneath it, weak, but a good sign that morning had come. She heaved the door open, desperate for the autumn sunlight to wash away the dirt and blood that stained her thoughts.

Autumn did not greet her.

The forest had crystallised during the night. The leaves and grass had been dusted with starlight, sharpening them like knives that glinted in the sun. Autumn had vanished, and though the sun would soon melt the land-scape back into what it had been, winter was nipping at its heels.

Penny forcefully exhaled, and watched a cloud of her breath swirl in the air. Her heart skipped a beat.

There was no longer any time to waste.

The first frost had come.

Penny rushed inside, her breathing a pained hiss. She scrambled for her things – the clothing, blankets and all the food she had managed to scrounge from the house – and shoved them into the first plastic bag she could find. Then she forced herself out into the cold.

The chilled morning air was like a heavy slap to the face, but the physical aspect she could deal with. It was the knowledge of what was soon to happen that scared her. In a week's time, a small, rick-ety wooden bridge would be lifted up and pulled away from the large chasm in the rock it balanced over.

Penny swore under her breath and batted the visions away.

She had plenty of time.

She took a step towards the trees, aiming for the area she had last spoken with Samantha, and then she faltered. Samantha wouldn't be there anymore, would she?

An uncomfortable prickle of anger crept up her arms.

No.

Samantha had what she wanted now, and she had abandoned her to get it.

Left her to die.

Of course she had. Everybody abandoned her in the end.

Mary, Samantha, her fath—

A branch snapped somewhere in the distance. Penny clenched the muscles in her body until she was almost trembling with the force of keeping herself still. When seconds passed and there was no further sound, she allowed her body to relax. She brushed dirty hair from her forehead, and then stared around her.

To her right, a small dirt path could just be seen edging into the forest. It was as good a place to start as any, she supposed. Penny placed her plastic bag into a blanket, rolled it twice over, and then tied each end around her body. She wrapped the second blanket around her shoulders and then stared into the forest, arms crossed and fingernails pushed into the bruised skin of her biceps.

Penny didn't need Samantha and her stupid sister. She didn't need their dirty dog to search for water or to warn her about… them.

Penny didn't need anyone else, she never had.

She would find the river, find the house before the bridge was raised, and then she would find Mary.

And she would get back to her son.

She would not be stopped. Not by anyone or anything.

Not anymore.

Penny fell to all fours as her stomach lurched. She heaved twice, shivering with sudden cold, and then watched as foul liquid shot up out of her throat and onto the grass in front of her.

The feeling of relief was quickly followed by another lurch. Vomit came again, burning her nose and stinging her eyes. The sour scent of it overwhelmed her. She heaved again, but this time her stomach no longer had anything to expel. Penny spat onto the grass, hoping to rid herself of the taste but achieving nothing except a drier mouth. She rolled away from the vomit, onto her side, slick with sweat and still trembling.

The sickness had come over her not long after she entered the forest. At the time, Penny assumed it was just due to lack of food and water. Frustrated to be losing time, she stopped to eat – a few thin strips of salted unknown meat, and a small handful of dry, stale rice. It had helped for a little while, and Penny pushed herself further into the foliage, harder than she probably should have. The sun had been warm against her back when the shivering began. That had been the first sign of something being badly wrong.

A churning in her stomach quickly followed the shivering.

Penny pulled at one of the corners of the blanket wrapped around her and wiped the vomit and sweat from her face.

'I'm just pushing myself too hard,' she huffed, pulling herself upright with shaky hands. 'All I need is a bit of rest.'

But she couldn't rest.

Not when she knew how little time there was left. If she was lucky, there would be no more frosts, and the bridge would stay in place for another few weeks. If she was unlucky…

Penny shakily rose to her feet, the metal bar holding most of her weight. In front of her were two trees, twisted together until nearly inseparable. Their foliage was still mostly green, almost untouched by autumn. Between the leaves, in the distance, Penny could see some sort of clearing.

She smiled through her pain, a strange grimace on a mud-streaked face. A clearing had to be a good sign. It might not be the river, but it had to be something, at least. She pushed forward, through the trees, through the thick brambles that scratched her already throbbing foot and bruised skin.

Her pace quickened as the dim forest filled with light from the clearing. She was hungry for it. Eyes blurred and stinging from the sweat that drenched her face, she stumbled on a root, yelped, and fell into the clearing.

Panting, she brought her head up from the grass in which she lay. Penny wanted to scream, but the sound caught in her throat, along with her breath. Her chest heaved, not with nausea, but with a single painful sob.

She did not have the energy to keep herself from crying.

The little stone house that had belonged to Harry and Olivia, the little stone house she had spent who knows how long trapped within, the little stone house she had been trying to run from, stood defiantly in front of her.

Mocking her.

She had been so sure of the way, so sure she could make it on her own, only to find she had been going in circles.

Penny found her voice, and let out an almighty scream. She screamed until the breath was gone, until the sound crumbled away as her body failed to keep up with her pain.

Her head sank back down into the grass.

Everything hurt.

It hurt so much.

She no longer had the strength or will to move.

Maybe the sound would draw those monsters to her.

Maybe that would be best.

They would grab her and cling to her until her skin fell away and she was only a pile of bones.

She should have drowned herself in the river.

Mary's face faded in and out of her mind.

Smiling.

Smirking.

Penny wanted to destroy her, more than anything.

Ruin her and tear her to pieces.

But there was no chance of that anymore.

She was lost, completely and utterly, and there was not enough strength left inside of her to stumble around in circles for hours on end, hoping to get lucky. If Samantha hadn't left her, if she hadn't selfishly abandoned her to get her sister back, Penny might have had a chance. Without her, she had nothing.

Penny moaned quietly into the dirt.

A single loud snap, close by to her left. Penny rolled to her side and stared into the trees. The sun was still bright in the sky; it had been clear and cloudless all day.

Another snap. Definitely something moving, but what? It was far too bright out to be one of the creatures, unless they had suddenly learned some new tricks.

An animal then. Wouldn't that be funny? Left to die in a forest filled with those monsters, only to be eaten alive by a bear. Or a wolf.

Penny rolled from her side onto her back, closed her eyes and waited for death.

The snap came again, no closer than it had been before. This time, however, it was followed by a small, sad, whine.

Penny's eyes shot open.

She had misheard.

She was imagining things.

She had to be.

It wasn't possible.

Was it?

She rolled to her front, pushed up onto her feet. She hobbled over to the noise, one painful step after the other. Her body screamed with pain but she had to know. Had to see.

She stumbled into the thick forest, following the whines and yelps, moving closer and closer to a familiar copse of trees.

Penny pressed herself against a particularly thick trunk, and then swivelled around it.

In front of her was the tree she had sat on with Samantha at her side, on the day she had left for the house. In the trunk, carved with a heavy hand, was a single word.

Sorry.

Beneath it, tied to the tree with a long, thick rope, was Samantha's dog.

At the sight of Penny the dog sprang to his feet, tail wagging, and searched around. Searching for Samantha, she supposed. Warily, Penny moved closer to the dog, and then placed her hand on his head.

'I'm sorry,' she said to the dog, meaning every word. 'She's left you too. I'm really sorry.'

The dog continued to look, craning his head around Penny to see beyond her. His tail wagged slower and slower, and eventually did not move at all. With another whine, the dog laid himself back down beside the tree. Penny shuffled over to him and collapsed onto the ground herself, leaning her back against the trunk. She slowly stroked the dog's fur.

The dog lifted his head and laid it across her lap.

They sat together, against the tree, until the sun had moved so far across the sky it would have been impossible for Penny to set off for the river. It would have been dark by the time she got anywhere at all. Instead, she would need to waste yet another night in the house. She looked over to the dog, fast asleep beside her, and then bit her lip.

A small part of her, one she hadn't even been aware of, wanted to let the dog go. He was smart, she had seen him, he was bound to be able to find his way home. Back to his master. It would be unfair of her to keep him with her.

Then again, the dog was her only chance of finding the river and of getting home. She needed him. Besides, did Samantha really deserve to have him back? She had her sister now, after all, and Penny had no one.

Would the dog even listen to her?

The thoughts went round and round in her head, chasing each other, fighting and bickering. She was getting nowhere.

'Look,' she said aloud. The dog's ears twitched, but otherwise he did not move.

'Samantha's gone. She's gone. And I need you. I'm sorry. You need to come with me, okay?' She rose to her feet and began pulling at the rope that kept the dog tied to the tree. The dog stood also, staring at her with his deep brown eyes.

The rope came free, and Penny grabbed at it before the dog could make his escape. He pulled against the rope, and then looked back at her. He whined.

'No,' Penny said. 'No, she's gone.'

The dog pulled again. Penny pulled back, and took a step towards the house.

The dog turned to her, baring his teeth and beginning to growl.

'Gnash your teeth together all you want, I don't care. I'm sorry, but I really don't.'

The dog growled louder.

Penny pulled again. The dog dug his paws into the dirt, continuing to gnash his teeth as Penny dragged him to the house. Eventually he stopped pulling and began to walk alongside her, though whether he had given up or just felt sorry for her, she wasn't sure.

She crept into the house quietly, pausing to make sure of the silence. When nothing came running out at her from the shadows within, she shut the door, released the dog, and slid slowly to the floor. Penny reached over and tenderly stroked her foot.

The bandages were wet again.

She sighed.

The dog sat down in front of her and snorted, spraying her with snot.

'Hey, this isn't my fault,' Penny muttered, wiping her face in distaste. 'I wasn't the one who left you here.'

The dog continued to stare. Penny sighed again and took off her makeshift rucksack. From the folds of the fabric she took out several pieces of meat. She shoved most into her mouth, chewing loudly, and then reluctantly threw the rest to the dog. He sniffed the food, and then began to eat. Penny hoped the food would make him a little more receptive to her, but really she doubted it would have any effect at all.

'So what's your name then?' she said, watching the dog devour the strip of meat. 'I never heard her call you anything. Do you even have a name?'

The dog finished the food, and then began sniffing at the ground. As he came across a mound of dust he drew back, eyes closed, teeth gnashing together, and then he sneezed.

Penny laughed quietly.

'Even when you sneeze, you're gnashing your teeth. That'll wear them down, you know.'

She smiled.

'I was gonna call you "Stupid", but I guess "Nash" works just as well. Better, probably. You're not really all that stupid, are you?'

The dog snorted in reply, yawned, and settled back down to the floor.

Penny remained motionless for the rest of the afternoon, growing more nervous as the light faded into the evening. Shadows swallowed the top of the staircase, blotting it from view. Penny tried not to picture the bodies lying above, tried not to imagine what would happen to her if they turned out to be anything other than dead. She moved only when she found she needed to urinate, and after relieving herself she crept back into the hallway, choosing to lay close to the dog, instead of facing the stairs as she had been before. Nash looked up as she shuffled next to him, and then placed his head onto her thighs.

A bead of sweat rolled down past her temple. She casually wiped it away, and scratched the dog gently behind the ear.

They slept beside each other in the hallway that night, backs to the staircase and to the bodies of two people that lay motionless in the dark. Backs to the body floating in water surrounded by fading candlelight. Penny woke several times, sure she could hear movement from the floor above.

Someone dragging themselves down the staircase.

She almost wished she had spent the night in the cold, dark forest, but upon looking at the dog, his mouth open slightly as he breathed, she was rather glad she hadn't.

Chapter Fourteen

Penny leaned her head across the top of the metal pipe, closing her eyes and resisting the urge to scream. The rope, wrapped tightly around her right hand, was pulled taut.

'Please. For the love of God, please. Show me where the damn river is.'

She looked up. Nash, slouched on a mound of fallen leaves, yawned.

It had taken all morning to get this far, just beyond where she had found the dog in the first place. Initially Nash had bounded along at her side, pulling her onward with excitement. Penny had been naive enough to hope her peace offering the previous night had led to a truce between them, until the dog realised he was not being taken to Samantha. Then the trouble had begun.

Penny had tried everything she could think of to make Nash move. He ate the food he gave her, would stand and sit on command, but otherwise would not budge an inch.

Penny pushed her head into the bar, hoping the pain would clear her mind or at least provide some momentary distraction from the frustration. If they didn't set off soon, they would have to spend another night in the house. She could not afford to lose yet another day.

Penny straightened up and pulled at the rope, testing it.

'Please, you stupid, stinking, worthless dog. You found water for Samantha; I know you can damn well do it.'

The dog sat up straight. Cocked his head.

His eyes were bright and alert.

Penny allowed herself a grin.

'About time. Come on you dumb thing, what word got you moving? Samantha?'

No reaction. She tried again.

'Water? Was it water?'

The dog rose to his feet and began to sniff at the ground, slowly moving away from their location and into the grabbing branches of the forest around them. He stopped, ears and tail rigid as he stared into the distance. Then he started to pull.

Penny, despite the pain and the fatigue, smiled as they scrambled through the trees.

'She's always hated me, Nash. She was born before me, but not by much. Not compared to the others. She always thought she was better than everyone else. The way she looked through you as if you weren't there. I think she hated the fact that I was around and she couldn't have all the special attention a child gets to herself. She probably wanted it to be me on the other side of the door that day. Wouldn't put it past her. What do you think?'

Penny lifted a branch out of the way of her face and ducked under it. The dog ran around the trunk of the tree and peed, managing to wrap the rope around it in the process. Penny unwound the rope, waited for the dog to re-adjust to his location, and then followed behind when he began to move again.

'I guess it must have been annoying for her – wanting to have been better than everyone else, wanting to be that special child, and then suddenly another child comes crashing into the house. Knowing that no matter what she did now, she would never be quite that important again. It's sad really. Not an excuse, but sad. Know what I mean?'

The dog did not reply. He had found a hole beneath some tree roots, and stuck his head inside. Penny tugged gently at the rope and the dog pulled himself away, nose covered in a dusting of dirt.

They had started walking in silence, Penny carefully holding her blanket bag against her chest to make as little noise as possible, and stepping carefully to muffle the sound. But as the day brightened, cool and clear, she grew tired of silence. What did it matter if she was stuck in the forest? Or if the clouds suddenly covered the sky and one of the false ones heard her? She was tired of being quiet, tired of running and hiding. She didn't have the energy to care anymore. And so, out of defiance, she began to talk.

She started with the weather.

'It's getting cold, Nash,' or, 'Do you think it will rain, Nash? We'll need to find shelter.' Eventually she had started describing the house, its many old, stale corridors and old stale inhabitants. She told him about her father and the day he had left her. That had brought the topic to Mary.

'She's always wanted a child,' Penny said, swinging her good leg over a rock, and then sliding the other carefully behind. 'Even when we were children it was all she would talk about. I think she thought because she had been born it somehow made her magically immune to whatever abnormality had affected the rest of the world. She married Lewis, but no babies. No surprises there. Must have been a real shocker when I popped one out. Beating her for the second time. She's probably got her disgusting claws into *my* kid now, though. Got him wrapped right around her little finger.'

The dog sniffed at something in a bush, then sneezed.

'You're right,' said Penny. 'Doesn't matter. We're on our way back now.'

It was freeing, in a way. Being able to talk out loud about all the little nasty thoughts in her head. She could tell the dog anything without having to worry about consequences. It also helped her to think. As the day wore on, she had found her thoughts becoming muddled, sentences turning into nothing. It was easier talking out loud somehow.

They stopped to eat at a fallen tree, its bark still damp from the morning. Penny perched herself on top of it and pulled out the few bags of food she had managed to scrounge from the house. There was little meat left, and so she licked at some sweet powder with a dry tongue instead. In her haste she had forgotten to grab any sort of water rations, not that she would have had anything to carry it in. She twisted in her seat, arm outstretched, and grabbed a handful of leaves from the low branches of the tree beside her. Some were dry, but others were cool and moist to the touch. She squeezed them over her waiting mouth. The few foul-tasting droplets that landed within were not worth the effort.

'We need to find that river soon,' she said, opening her palm and watching the leaf mulch fall to the ground. She shoved Nash with a foot, gently. 'Can't you hurry up?'

The dog licked his lips.

Penny sighed, and pulled out a strip of meat from the bag. She scowled and threw it to Nash, who finished it in two quick bites.

Her pace was slowing. She realised it a while back, but pushed it from her mind. Now it was impossible to ignore. Her tongue was dry enough to stick to the roof of her mouth, and the pain in her foot had become an unrelenting companion. Her body ached and trembled. Her skin burned, despite the cold.

She needed to be close to the river, to the house. There was only so much more she could take. She needed something to quench her thirst or she wouldn't survive. But she had no idea how much further there was to go, or even if they were heading in the right direction.

'All these stupid trees look the same,' she mumbled, fighting against a violent shiver.

The dog looked up, cocked his head.

Penny sighed.

'Never mind. Let's just go. Water, Nash. Find the water.'

She slid to her feet, not even stopping to wince at the pain in her foot. There would be time for that later.

Her heart pounded in her ears, and at her feet the dog sniffed and snorted. They were the only sounds she could make out, the rustling of the trees having been pushed to background noise several hours back. Every footstep made her entire body throb, from her head down. So she wasn't surprised when she didn't hear the rushing of water until they were close enough to notice the increase of moisture in the air.

The dog stopped in front of her, nose to the sky, and then bounded off to the right fast enough to pull the rope from her hands. Penny raced after him, struggling to keep up, and constantly pulling her bag back onto her shoulder. She called out, swearing loudly at the dog as he ran out of sight.

Penny ducked under a branch, edged around a shrub and froze.

She grinned, threw the bag to the ground, limped out of the forest, and into the warm sunlight.

Over to the glistening, gurgling river.

She pulled off her dirty, smelly clothes, placed them on a rock and slowly waded into the icy water. The ripples and waves lapped at her hot skin, soothing it. The water was so cold it almost hurt, but once Penny was waist deep she took a breath and dived completely under. Beneath the surface she rubbed at her skin and hair, only surfacing when her chest began to tighten with the lack of oxygen. Above the surface she took an almighty breath, then lowered her mouth to the water and drank until her teeth ached.

She looked over to the dog, who was still at the water's edge and, having drunk his fill, was bouncing and barking at the waves coming towards him.

'Hey, Nash,' Penny called, waving an arm out of the water. 'Aren't you coming in? You a wimp?'

The dog edged forward, and then darted back as another wave came closer. He barked.

'Big wimp,' Penny muttered, and waded back through the current to the riverside.

The dog ran at her, licking at the water on her legs until she was forced to push him aside. She pulled on her shorts and vest, water still running across her skin, and began to scour the water's edge for anything she could use. A little way down from where they had emerged she found a dirty bottle with its lid intact. She cleaned it as best she could and then filled it with water. She placed it in the bag, and turned to call the dog away from the river when she noticed he was standing rigid, hair on end, and growling at something on the other side.

Slowly, Penny looked up.

Across the water, between the trees, stood a small, white figure, long hair dancing in the breeze. Childlike. Smiling. Wrong.

The thing from Olivia's house.

The thing in the bath.

The girl.

The false girl.

It had followed.

It had survived, and it had found her.

'It's sunny,' Penny whispered, eyes wide. 'The river is bright. It can't see me. It can't. It can't.'

Penny stepped to the right. The thing's head followed her, its smile growing.

Penny couldn't breathe.

The dog whined.

Had Olivia been telling the truth? Had the creature been… changed?

The thing stepped forward, placing a tiny foot into the river. Penny edged back, hand searching blindly for anything she could use as a weapon. Finding nothing.

The thing took another step, both feet now in the water.

The dog barked.

The thing cocked its head, stretched its face wider, and then, slowly, took a step back.

Away from her.

Whether river or dog had stopped it, Penny didn't care. It was all the chance she needed. She screamed towards the creature, animal-like and guttural, then grabbed her bag and ran.

Her foot didn't matter.

The dog didn't matter.

She needed to go.

Needed to get away.

Her vision swam. Her chest burned. Penny heard a snort and risked a glance over her shoulder. The dog had followed and was trailing close behind. In the distance was the creature. It was in the same place, watching. Smiling. Motionless.

'Rot there you bitch,' Penny spat, her voice barely audible above her own heavy breaths as she hid herself deeper within the trees.

It was not long before Penny spotted the hill.

It came upon them all of a sudden, peeking above the tree line on the opposite side of the river. It was probably further than it looked, but just seeing it filled her with a dizzying storm of emotions – hope, relief, determination.

Dismay.

She would eventually need to cross the river, a treacherous task in itself even without Olivia's monster lurking on the other side. Once she had crossed, she would be in constant danger.

Deep in her gut, she was convinced the creature was following her, despite the sun. She didn't want to think about what would happen if it found her.

Penny and Nash followed the river, hiding in the trees but keeping it in sight at all times.

She was rattled and wary, jumping at every little sound, but a part of her was euphoric. She had looked one in the eye, watched it come towards her, and then fall back. One of those things had seen her, and she had survived.

'Suck on that, Mary,' she mumbled under her breath.

The hill was more of a jagged cliff than the hills described by her father in stories: a sharp mass of rock and dirt with the river cutting through it. She could follow the river all the way to the top if she wanted. It was a safe route, often used by scouting parties, but it was a long one. Too long. By the time she got to the peak, the bridge would be long gone.

She would need to take the clearing that lay beyond the trees.

'It's fine,' she said, as the dog whined at her. 'We'll get there. No problem. Move faster, Nash.'

Better not to think about it.

To take her mind off things Penny began to fuel herself on memories, anything that would stoke the fire of her hatred. The hatred that was keeping her moving forward.

She recalled all the times Mary had ignored her in the hallways, all the dark looks across the dining hall and the muttered insults under her breath. She remembered a dark evening, talking with friends in the library when Mary had entered. Mary had caused a fuss and then started to cry, of course. Penny had been blamed and her friends had all left her.

Who needed friends anyway?

The sun broke from between the gathering grey clouds, creating a silver shimmer across the river's surface. Penny smiled, and remembered spending sunny days with her son by the river. On one such day, she had placed him in his makeshift high chair in order to quickly fetch him another cloth nappy. When she returned, Mary was holding her son, her child, rocking him against her chest, smiling as if she had every right to be happy near anything that belonged to Penny. As if she had any right to touch her son.

Penny had marched over to her, pulled her son from the woman's arms and slapped her across the face before she'd even opened her mouth to explain herself.

'How dare you,' Penny had hissed at her, face burning. The older woman stared at her feet, turning pale.

'I saw him on his own. He could have been hurt. I just—'

'How *dare* you?'

'I was just looking after him. I didn't mean to—'

'What, he fell out of his chair and into your arms? How lucky for you.'

'He looked sad. I just wanted to—'

'Oh, I know what you wanted.'

Penny had stepped up to her and leaned down, making sure their eyes were level.

'If you ever touch him again, I'll cut your fingers off. Do you understand?'

Penny paused beside a tree, the dog panting beside her. She frowned.

In the past that memory had always made her feel good. It was her evidence, proof that Mary had been out to get her, to steal everything she had. Why was it that now she could only see Mary's smile while holding her son? The broken look on her face as Penny had stormed off with him?

Penny slapped her head, as if to knock out the strange thoughts.

The dog looked at her, his ears up.

'Shut up,' said Penny, pushing past him. She walked to the river's edge, over sharp stones and broken branches, and stared across to the other side.

'You know what? It seems narrower here, and I'm sick of this forest. We're crossing. Come on.'

She threw her blanket into the bag, filling up all the remaining space and leaving no room for her clothes. She would have to wear them into the river and dry them on the other side. She sighed and began to wade once more into the icy water. Behind her she heard a cry, and she turned, frowning at the dog who was still pacing nervously on the riverbank.

'You can swim or you can stay there. Your choice.'

Nash cried again, and tapped at the water with his front paw. Penny ignored him and lifted the bag over her head in order to stop the water from soaking into the blanket. She held onto it with one arm, using the other to paddle as the water became deeper.

'Just keep kicking,' she said to herself, spitting out a mouthful of water. Behind her came a splash. Nash had apparently decided to come after all.

She pushed further into the water, and suddenly her body moved of its own accord. She was caught in the current, and though weaker than it had been a few days ago, it was still strong enough to pull her far from her original starting point before she managed to hold herself against a nearby rock. The splashing behind her had come to a stop.

Penny had to shout to be heard over the water.

'If you've already made it to the other side I'm going to be so—'

But the dog was nowhere to be seen.

Not on either side of the river.

Not in the water.

Penny's blood turned to ice.

She pushed herself away from the rock and into the current.

'Damn it. Where are you, Nash?'

Waves lashed at her face, blinding her. The bag grew heavier. It was soaking up the water. She needed to get to the other side if she wanted to save the food.

'Damn it. Damn it. Nash, come here!'

Behind her, a splash. Only momentarily, but enough. Penny swam with the current, allowing it to take her further downstream and push her beneath the surface several times. While under, she forced her eyes open, and saw a long dark shape in the near distance.

Penny surfaced, inhaled and dived under again.

She pushed herself closer to the shape, until she was finally close enough to catch the dog by his fur, pulling him to her chest. He did not struggle. Did not move. Penny wrapped an arm around him but it wasn't enough. She twisted her other arm to get a better grip and cried out. Her scream was silent beneath the surface.

She had dropped the bag. Her food, her supplies, her blankets – gone. If she hurried she might just be able to find it, but if she let go of Nash, he would die.

She was running out of air.

She needed to make a choice.

The dog or the food.

Penny screamed again, and then pulled the dog up towards the surface. She struggled out of the water onto the rocky riverside, dragging him alongside her until he was secure on the ground.

Nash did not move.

'Come on, get up. Don't make me regret this.'

She shook the dog roughly and hit him on the back like she had once seen an elder do to a man choking.

Water spilled from the dog's mouth. He rolled to his front, heaved up more water, and dropped his head down as if it were too heavy for him to hold.

Penny scratched the dog gently behind the ear and fell beside him, exhausted.

'How you doing, you stupid thing?'

The dog licked at her hand, and Penny quickly decided that the bag would have been too heavy to carry all the way home anyway.

Penny hung her clothes over a branch to dry, peeling them away from her damp skin. Then she sank to the ground, pulling the dog onto her lap and wrapping her arms around him. They were both drenched through, and the dog shivered violently next to her. She squeezed him tighter, lying her head gently on top of his.

Penny was in pain. Her foot ached, and the bandage was soaked through with nothing available to replace it. With one hand, she stroked the dog's fur, and began to sing under her breath with a raspy voice.

'Hush little baby, don't say a word. Mummy's gonna buy you a mockingbird.'

Her voice cracked.

She couldn't get any further.

As the sky darkened and her stomach growled with hunger, she hugged her friend and together they shivered in the wind.

Chapter Fifteen

The ground was white with frost, sparkling like light kissing a clear surface of water. It was beautiful, and Penny hated it.

Every moment seemed to bring with it colder air, wind that stung her face and caused her teeth to chatter. It froze her cold, wet clothes to her skin until she could feel the ice in her bones.

She would reach the edge of the forest soon.

It had to be close.

They had begun walking at sunrise, immediately after waking. They had no reason to stop and eat, after all. Nash had been cautious at first, plodding along at her side so slow she worried the river had hurt him more than she first realised. It had taken the sudden appearance of a squirrel to knock him out of it, and soon he was running ahead at such a pace she struggled to keep up.

The ground, which had been thick sloppy mud first thing in the morning, started to dry. It became rocky, almost dusty in places and Penny regained strength at the sight of it.

She was getting closer.

Penny grinned at the thought, her teeth clenched tightly enough to cause her jaw to ache, and then jumped excitedly from one foot to the other without thinking.

Her foot hit the ground, but may as well have been smashed against a sharp boulder from a great height.

She shrieked and her leg buckled, sending her tumbling to the ground. Penny breathed in dirt, tasted it against her tongue, but couldn't bring herself to move. Trembling, she lay for several minutes, until Nash pushed his wet nose against her cheek. Wrapping an arm around his neck, she managed to pull herself upright.

Penny looked down at her foot, bulging out of the sandal, and swallowed the rising bile shooting up her throat. Her foot, once a shiny red, had turned an angry, deep purple. The wound itself was now almost black at its centre, framed with a thick yellow crust that flaked beneath her touch. She tried to clean the pus in the river, wiping away the thick crust, but the wound had begun to leak again almost immediately and so she left it to ooze.

She didn't dare create a bandage – even the wind brushing against her raw skin made her eyes water.

Her foot was not getting better, and that was beginning to frighten her.

When the nausea subsided and she caught her breath, Penny stumbled to her feet and immediately began walking. There was no longer any time for pity, she needed to keep moving and that was what she did.

Get up, brush off, move on.

She walked, and walked, and then the forest started to end. Trees became shrubs, and shrubs became tall patches of grass. Penny could hear the river somewhere to her right, the cool smell of water filling her mouth with the little saliva she had left. She placed her hand against a tree as she stepped around a large rock, and then paused.

In front of her, close enough to touch, was her hill. Her home. Her lips trembled with the swell of emotion that came over her, but she did not move.

Between her and home, her son, and revenge, was an open clearing – a large empty expanse of grass and rock that sloped up towards the house.

Penny hesitated at the edge of it, building up her courage. Once she stepped out of the cover of the trees she would be entirely out in the open. It was very likely she was already being pursued by Olivia's sinister hybrid. Once darkness fell, she would be completely vulnerable. To get home safely, she would need to climb the slope before the sun set.

She would need to walk without stopping.

'We can reach it by nightfall. Definitely.'

Nash whined.

Penny found she couldn't help but agree, but what else was she supposed to do?

She took a breath, exhaled, and then stepped out onto the cold, white grass.

The river came back into view not long after they had entered the clearing, and they followed it up the slope towards home. Penny liked having it in her line of sight. The sound was comforting to her, and it was nice to be near clean water. Every time her stomach screamed out for food, she simply paused to take a drink. It didn't ease the growing pain in her stomach, but it helped take her increasingly clouding mind off it for just a little while.

Besides, it was probably best to stay away from food. *Starve a fever, feed a cold.* The voice of her father.

Or was it the other way around?

Penny began to pant, her breath escaping her mouth as thin, wispy clouds. She watched them weave through the air as she shivered, and sweat, hot and cold, came over her in waves. Several times her vision turned to snow, and she was forced to cling to Nash in order to stay upright.

Every time she placed her foot on the ground it was like standing on hot coals, and by the time the sun had risen as high as the hill in front of her she could think of nothing but the pain. She tried trailing her foot in the icy river water as she walked, tried limping and crawling. Nothing eased the agony.

Then her thoughts changed.

She began to fantasise about removing the foot entirely.

Cutting it off, biting it off.

Anything.

She wasn't fussy.

She just knew that if her foot was gone, the pain would be gone also.

The hill moved closer, and then farther away. Penny thought she was getting nearer, could see herself walking past rocks which had to mean she wasn't staying still, but sometimes it seemed as though she had passed the same rock more than once.

Perhaps she was merely walking in circles.

'The river is moving,' she mumbled. 'It's tricking me.'

When she stopped for lunch, a belly-filling gulp of water that made her lips numb, she started to see the flies.

One landed on her arm as she pulled her head up from the water and she swatted it away in distaste, only for it to land again on her thigh. She cupped her hands and splashed water over her burning face, letting the droplets trickle down her chin and onto her neck. When she brought her hands back down from her mouth, there were two flies crawling over her fingers.

Penny wrinkled her nose and shook her hands. The flies darted off, whizzing in the air and creating trails in the sky.

Three flies landed on her knee.

'They'll leave once I start moving,' she said, voice echoing in her head. She stumbled to her feet, grabbing the dog to help, and began to limp back towards where she thought the hill was.

The flies, unable to perch on her body, began to fly about her head. She saw them everywhere, black dots moving in the corner of her eyes, whirling in front of her.

To and fro.

Back and forth.

In and out.

Sometimes there was only one and sometimes she would walk through a cloud of them. She would have to close her mouth otherwise she would swallow them, and they would crawl over her tongue, down her throat and beneath her skin forming pulsing lumps that itched like hell until they burst and more, more, more flies came tumbling out.

At one point she got lost in a fly cloud, and when it dissipated the hill had vanished.

She was facing the other direction. Going the wrong way.

'The hill keeps moving.' She laughed, desperately.

Behind her, in the distance, at the other side of the clearing, were two more flies.

Little flies.

Big flies.

Sometimes one bigger than the other.

They were following her.

Gaining on her.

She spun back around, back towards the hill.

The sun had started to set.

She was not any closer.

Penny was reluctant to walk in the dark, but just as reluctant to fall asleep out in the open. She stood still, swaying, unsure about what option would be least likely to kill her. Eventually Nash decided for her, and lay down in exhaustion behind a particularly large rock. Penny limped over and fell next to him.

Her vision grew hazy.

The flies were back.

She couldn't see through them this time.

Was there a person behind them?

No, two people, grey and ugly.

Fly people.

The two flies that had been following her had found her.

They were abominations – hairy and grey. But she knew their voices.

Mary.

Her son.

'You're flies,' Penny said, laughing at the creatures, their large green eyes iridescent.

She could see herself in them. She looked awful. How funny.

The larger fly, Mary, twitched her head, and began to speak in a voice that hummed with distortions.

'You're going to kill me,' she said.

'Sure am.'

'Why?'

'I hate you.'

'Why?'

'You left me out here. All alone,' said Penny, in a sing-song voice.

Mary twitched again, flies falling away from her spiky skin like ash.

'Why?' said Mary. Voice echoing.

'Why?' she said again. It wasn't just her voice this time, but that of Penny's son too. They buzzed together in unison.

'Because you want to kill me. You hate me. Always have.'

The figures distorted, came apart and back together again.

'Why?' they said together. As one. She hated that. 'Why? Why?'
'I don't know,' Penny screamed.

The figures shuddered and then started to crumble into mounds
of writhing insects, insects that flew away into the wind. Penny
reached out for what had been her son, but too late. The wind took
the insects away, and Penny was left alone with her dog and her pain.

She hunched her shoulders, lip trembling.

'Damn it,' she whispered, forcing herself back to her feet.

What did it matter what Mary thought. She was always out to
get her, even now.

She wanted her to stop.

To get caught.

Well, like hell would that happen.

Penny got up again and staggered over a rock, the dog whining
beside her as he rose shakily to his feet and plodded alongside her just
as slowly.

'She doesn't know anything,' she mumbled, her breath hot and
her mouth dry. 'Doesn't know anything about me. I hate her. I'll kill
her. You wait, I'll kill you. My foot hurts, Nash, it hurts. She had no
reason to do this. No reason. No reason.'

Buzzing around her ears, in her head.

'Lewis,' said the buzzing. 'That day by the river. I was always
alone. You made sure of that, didn't you?'

'Shut up,' Penny moaned.

'You had everything. You took everything.'

The voice increased in volume while lowering in pitch, dragging
the words.

Stretching them.

'You deserve to rot here.'

The flies landed on her face, crawling over her skin and pushing
their way into her hair. She thrashed at them, crying out. The flies
multiplied, crawling into her eyes until she could see nothing. The
buzzing in her head grew louder and louder.

Her legs buckled and she fell onto the grass.

I'm dying, she thought, and then began to laugh.

Something wet pressed against her cheek, and at first she thought it was the flies again. Penny began to hit her face, desperate to remove the insects, when she felt the wetness once more, this time accompanied by a low growl.

She opened her eyes.

The world was dark, and her breath caught in her throat in panic until she noticed moonlight shimmering on the river. The dog nudged her again, impatient.

'I'm up,' she said, pushing the dog away. 'I'm fine. Stop worrying.'

Again, the dog pushed her, then lowered his head and growled quietly. Penny's hand clenched against the dog's fur.

Something was wrong.

The air was different.

In the distance was a faint rustling, almost a whisper.

Penny hunched low, hiding herself in the tall grass, staying very, very still.

She shushed the dog when he growled again, and closed her eyes, trying to pinpoint the source of the sound.

It could have been mistaken for wind, had the grass been anything but as still as the dead. The noise was deep, breathy.

Melodic.

A song.

Someone was singing.

Her brain muddy with sleep, Penny's first thought was that Mary had come after her. Had come to stop her, devour her before she could reach the house and take her revenge.

The voice drew closer.

The song grew clearer.

Penny knew that song.

As she heard it, a memory made up of smoke and hands and teeth filled her head.

It was not a woman's voice.

It was a man's.

That man's.

Penny hunched lower to the ground.

He was partially to blame.

If he hadn't been around, she wouldn't have used him to hurt Mary.

If he hadn't been around, Mary wouldn't have cast her out.

It was his fault.

Penny tensed and licked her lips.

He moved closer.

Penny tried to pull at the dog, but she could no longer feel him. He had gone.

Didn't matter.

He wasn't important.

Penny listened and waited.

The man stopped mere metres from her and turned around in the moonlight. His entire skin was swollen and black, his lips crusted over with blood and teeth stained red. The man stopped singing and started to mumble. His eyes were half-closed in the darkness.

'I saw her,' he said. 'I saw her, baby. It's okay, it's okay. You'll wake up, once she's back, you'll wake up. Hold Daddy's hand.'

Penny, heart pounding in her throat, searched for any other sign of movement but could see nothing.

He was alone.

The man swayed on the spot.

'She's here. I saw her. I know it. I know it. I—'

He fell backward and hit the ground with a sickeningly wet thump. When the sound died, Penny rose to her feet and walked over to him, slowly.

Carefully.

He was still conscious, staring at her wildly, eyes bulging. How had he come so far? He had died. She had watched him die. Hadn't she?

'Hello, Lewis,' she said.

He smiled wide, running his thick, swollen tongue over his lips. A chunk of dried blood crumbled away as he touched it, and he swallowed it down.

'I knew it,' he whispered. 'I knew I'd find you. I was so far behind, really far, but I found you. Saw you. So lucky. Missed you. Missed you. Kiss me, please.'

'I can't do that, Lewis.'

A large rock was pressed up against her foot, almost as though it had been planned. Penny bent down, and rubbed it slowly between her hands.

'You were just as bad as she was,' she said, lifting the rock above her head.

Lewis grinned.

His eyes were black, and flies fell from his mouth as he spoke.

'You were worse,' he buzzed.

Penny screamed at him, tensed her arms ready to bring the rock crashing down into his skull.

A cold wind licked at her neck and a long, raspy breath came out of the darkness behind her. Penny blinked.

The shape of Lewis crumbled away, becoming something else entirely.

Something smaller.

At her feet, where she thought Lewis had been, Nash cocked his head and whined quietly. Penny threw the rock away as if it had burned her fingers.

'I'm sorry,' she said, bringing her hands to her mouth. 'I'm so sorry, Nash. I didn't mean it. I didn't—'

The noise came again. Far away, but far too close.

'Haaaaaaa.'

The dog barked.

There was no time to worry about the dog.

Not anymore.

It was coming.

Chapter Sixteen

Penny did not stop running.

Not to catch her breath, or to quench her thirst.

Not to ease the burning pain crawling up her foot or to calm the flickering of her vision.

She had heard it.

Olivia's monster.

And if it was close enough to hear, it was close enough to see her. Catch her. Grab her, hold her, squeeze her, crush her, kill—

Penny pushed harder. If she stopped, she was dead.

She continued running, limping, and reached the hill at dawn. The scene might have been beautiful on any other sunrise – warm light creeping over grassy knolls and sharp pointed rocks that led skywards. But between sweat, tears and pain, her vision was blurry at best.

In front of her was something that appeared to be an old path, broken and steep like a staircase for giants, but beyond that she could only see distorted shapes and colours.

Penny, screaming with effort and bathed in sweat that ran like a river down her back, climbed. Every new rock she was forced to clamber over brought with it another growl from her throat.

Her hands slipped as they clung to rocks, or as she pushed Nash, who was still managing to keep up with her, over a particularly high ledge. Soon enough she found she had stopped screaming, and was just forcing herself on with her jaw set and her shoulders hunched.

Penny did not look back. She did not listen to the soft pattering of footsteps that seemed to follow her.

The climb became easier.

The rocks gave way to steep but manageable winding slopes, held together by rope-like roots of long dead plants. Soon it was barely a climb at all.

A cool breeze ruffled her hair and soothed her skin.

As the slope levelled out, Nash bounded past her, climbing over rocks and pushing his head into the small caverns that decorated the hillside, with a renewed energy. Penny couldn't help but smile, and the smile widened when she realised the sound of footsteps had been replaced by birdsong.

For the first time in hours, Penny stopped. She looked over her shoulder, back towards the way they had climbed, her legs tingling.

Nothing.

'Maybe they can't climb,' Penny whispered, doubting herself the moment the words left her lips. The house had been found once before, after all.

Maybe the creature had fallen, then. Or had finally succumbed to the light.

Maybe it was really gone.

Penny found herself smiling wider than she had in years. The smiles turned to laughter. Penny doubled over, clutching her stomach as her throat tightened and tears fell. Nash came over, barked happily, and then sniffed at her pocket.

Penny waved him away and wiped the tears from her face.

'Sorry, buddy. I don't have anything. I'll get you something good soon, I promise.'

She found a flat rock overlooking the long clearing and sat down, staring out towards the river that ran through it, glittering in the sun. The forest loomed at the edge of the field, its roots stretching out like fingers towards the grass. In a few years, the field would be gone entirely.

A bird chirped loudly behind her, and Penny looked over her shoulder, completely unsurprised.

'So, you followed me too,' she said to the little brown bird as it hopped along the edge of a flat rock. The bird tilted its head, hopped down onto the ground to peck for a while, and then fluttered back up to the rock. Penny sighed.

'I don't have anything to give you,' she said, watching the bird jump over to a boulder a little further away. 'But it's nice to see you again.'

The bird scurried across the rock, a large mountain of a thing that almost entirely obscured the view of the path they had taken. Penny smiled as the bird began to chirp at her.

Two small, grey hands reached up behind the rock either side of the bird. They waited a single moment, a single sharp breath, and then the hands closed.

Fingers laced.

The bird began to squeak.

Wings thumped against the hands, like a heartbeat. Penny's heartbeat.

She couldn't breathe.

The dog barked.

The sound of it brought her back to her senses. She screamed and forcefully grabbed the dog's fur, dragging him away despite his yelps. Penny shoved herself and the dog into a ditch, wrapped her arms around her friend and waited.

Trembling.

Heart pounding.

Each breath sliced through the silence as loud as thunder.

The thumping of the bird began to slow.

Until it just... Stopped.

Silence. A long, painful silence.

Penny waited.

And waited.

Her rage began to build.

She was hiding again.

Why was she always hiding?

She had not been brought up like this.

To hide in the dirt.

She was strong.

She needed to be strong.

Was she going to kill Mary, or would she hide from that too?

Pathetic.

She'd always been pathetic. Seething with jealousy at other people's happy lives.

Vindictive.

Desperate to ruin everyone.

A coward.

Penny, though her legs trembled and her blood rushed painfully in her ears, stood.

The thing, the monster in a child's form had its back to her. It was hunched, its grey skin almost like the stone of the hill. Its hair ruffled in the wind as it crushed the bird between its monstrous, black fingers.

It was distracted by the bird. It hadn't even noticed her stand.

Penny took a step towards it.

These things, these devils, had chased her all the way through the forest. They were the reason her foot bled and screamed at her in pain.

She took another step.

They were the reason she had been attacked by a pair of lunatics.

Another step.

They were the reason she had spent her whole damn life living in a house on a hill. In darkness and fear.

Another.

They were the reason she had met Mary, and the reason Mary had sent her to the forest.

They had ruined everything.

They had *started* everything.

And they had killed her father.

She clenched her fists, her teeth, her shoulders and then wailed, a dying animal screaming for its life.

She ran.

Not away from it, not this time.

It looked up away from the bird, large dark eyes settling on her face, but by then it was too late.

Penny's shoulder struck cold, hard skin. It resisted but she screamed again, pushing with every bit of rage she could drag to the surface.

She pushed until she reached the edge of the hill.

She pushed until the monstrous child rocked back and forth before the edge.

She pushed until it lurched over the side.

And she watched as it fell.

Penny howled at the creature as it bounced stiffly down the hillside, rolling in a cloud of dust. As she panted, her frantic brain, wired with rage and leftover adrenaline, took note of the fact the thing did not move at all.

Why would it?

It never moved once it had something in its grasp. Even as it tumbled it was completely motionless, still clutching its hands in front of it. Its eyes wide, blank, glassy. Its smile toothy, sharp and stretched.

Penny did not look away until the shape had vanished completely behind a sharp drop, and even then she did not move. The dog came up to her and licked her hand. Penny jumped and sank to her knees.

It was over. Surely, this time it was over.

Even Olivia's freak couldn't survive that.

From the bottom of the hill a small dark shape shot upwards into the sky. Penny flinched backward, and then smiled as the small brown bird flew into the clouds.

'No,' she said, gently rubbing the dog's neck. 'It's not over. Not yet.'

At the peak of the hill, close to the house, a deep dark crack ran through the rocky path. It had once been home to a sturdy stone bridge, wide enough for a vehicle to pass from the house into the forest, but the elders had torn it down immediately after they found it.

Too unsafe.

Too hard to keep watch.

Instead, the house-dwellers used wooden planks balanced across the gap to allow access to the beyond. Two men guarded the 'bridge' at all times throughout the day and were in charge of removing it before nightfall. They were under strict orders to only allow familiar faces to pass, and to remove the bridge at any sign of trouble, even if there were people still on the other side.

Two men were at the bridge now, one huddled beneath a thick wool jumper, rubbing his arms and staring out across the crevice. The other was looking up at the clouds above him, apparently bored out of his mind. He yawned loudly, and swore when the other man hit him on the back of the head.

'What the hell did you do that for?'

He turned to the man, glaring, but the other man was staring, slack-jawed, at the bridge. The man followed his gaze and found himself unable to speak a single word.

Penny, clinging onto consciousness, still had the strength to enjoy the look on their faces as she passed them. She held her head high, staring straight ahead as they crowded around her, hammering her with question after question. She ignored every single one, and limped onward. The dog stopped to sniff at one of the men's shoes, and then followed along behind.

As she rounded the corner, she heard one man say, 'I just can't believe it'.

As if there had ever been a chance of her not returning.

What did they take her for?

By the time she could smell burning meat coming from the house that loomed in front of her, she had only one thought in her mind, and it pulsed with each step. She was vaguely aware of people near her, clouded shapes in the corner of her eye whispering in groups, but that wasn't important.

She reached the large, wooden doors, pushed past the woman who stood in front of them, and then walked inside.

The hall smelled of old wood, dust and damp, and Penny's sandals clapped against the stone floor. The whispering grew louder, but she was no longer sure if the noise was coming from the people that surrounded her, or if the murmuring was a side effect of her fever. Maybe there were no people at all.

It didn't matter.

Nothing mattered.

As long as *she* was still here.

Penny walked to the end of the hall and looked up at the staircase. Steps upon steps. Almost endless.

It was nothing.

She gripped the banister and pulled herself up. Each step was like the pounding of a drum, in her head, in her foot, in her heart.

Her breathing became laboured, though not with exertion.

Her vision narrowed, blackening around the edges like a cavern.

All she could see was the top of the stairs.

That was all she needed.

Something brushed past her leg, and the feeling brought with it the vague recollection of a companion, a flickering thought at the edge of her mind that blew away instantly like a leaf in the wind.

Ten steps left. What were ten steps now?

The next floor was in view.

She was almost there.

Her feet placed themselves on the landing. Her body crawled to catch them up before they left without her.

Nothing hurt any more. Wasn't that funny?

The corridor seemed longer than before. It was a never-ending maze of doors and stale wallpaper. But it also seemed emptier. Colder.

Unreal.

The doors rushed past and the whispers grew louder.

She came to a stop outside a door, no different in size or shape to any of the others in the corridor.

Penny knew this door.

She had conceived her child there.

The child she could hear behind the door now.

A normal person may have cried, may have sunk to the ground at the sound of their child's voice, unheard for so long.

Penny did not cry.

She trembled in a rage great enough to blind her.

Her hand reached out and closed around the doorknob. Then, with her face white beneath the streaks of dirt and blood, Penny pushed the door open.

It was a sickeningly perfect sight.

Sunlight passed through the dark red curtains, casting a pink glow across the room and bathing everything in warmth.

Mary was sitting cross-legged on the floor. She was wearing a simple white dress and, for the first time since Penny had known her, had tied back her flat brown hair into a small knot on the top of her head. Her smile was wide, her cheeks red with joy. An expression of genuine happiness.

The grinning little boy sat opposite her, holding out his hands and pressing them to Mary's cheeks. He pushed, distorting Mary's face.

They laughed.

Penny saw grey hands clasp a bird, the beating of wings.

Her vision flickered.

Not yet.

Not yet.

She grabbed the door, which had opened silently, and slammed it against the wall. Mary, face still in the hands of the child, turned.

Her smile dropped and she blinked once, as if she were looking at a stranger.

Penny watched as Mary's expression changed, and drank in every emotion. First confusion, recognition, panic, dread and then horror.

She enjoyed that one best of all.

Mary said nothing. Did not scream, or try to explain. She just grabbed the boy and held him to her, cradling his head as if to protect him.

'You bitch,' said Penny, slurring her words. Her mouth didn't seem to be working properly.

She couldn't move her tongue.

Her vision pulsed and faded, becoming darkness and then sight once more.

She took a step into the room.

'You ruined my life. Took everything. Over and over and over...' She trailed off.

Mary again said nothing. She hid her face into the boy's shoulder, squeezing her eyes closed. Her neck was long and white. Penny reached out to strangle it.

She took another step forward, but she could no longer feel her feet. Her ankle buckled as she walked and Penny fell, screaming, before she was even close. Her foot began to cramp and each constriction was a hot blade in her skin, digging around in her flesh.

Her vision grew faint, grey and cloudy. The forest sky.

She screamed so loudly she did not hear Mary and the boy run from the room, and only realised she was alone when the door slammed shut behind them.

Before #5

They were arguing again. Not that there was ever a time recently when they weren't arguing.

They had actually started the morning quite pleasantly as far as Penny could tell. She had watched them from the shadows of the dining room doorway, staring as they laughed and smiled. Each smile was a punch in her gut, but she didn't have to endure it for long.

She never did.

Mary said something first, as always, but Penny didn't hear what. Lewis replied quickly, and soon the fight began in earnest, voices raised as the people surrounding them stared at the floor awkwardly.

Penny watched as Mary slammed down her plate of food, showering the table in oats. That was her cue.

Penny entered the room and stared about her as if she hadn't just spent the last hour snooping. She pretended to spot the pair, and waved to them. The couple grew silent, and after a few moments of glaring at each other, Lewis turned to Penny and offered her a small wave in return. Mary slapped his hand, but it was too late. Penny had already reached the table, smiling in as demure a fashion as she knew how.

She knew how pretty well.

'Lewis!' she said, loudly, wrapping her arms around his neck.

Mary and Lewis both flushed red for two very different reasons. Penny enjoyed them both.

'Hello, Penelope. Hi.'

'Oh, Penelope is far too formal. You've known me all my life, remember? It's Penny. I just wanted to thank you for your book recommendation.'

'Oh, no problem, Penelope. Uh, Pen. Sorry.'

Penny winced, but recovered quickly. Mary turned to her, her eyes dark and angry.

'Excuse me, *Penelope*, you're interrupting our breakfast.'

'We were only talking, Mary,' said Lewis, slowly pulling himself away from Penny's grasp. 'Only talking. Am I not allowed to talk to people now?'

Mary frowned at the table, pushing at her food with a faded metal spoon.

'I didn't say that.'

'Then why is this a problem?'

'Because it's always her. You're always talking to her.'

She pointed at Penny, who blinked like a child in return, as if she couldn't possibly know what Mary was talking about. As if she hadn't been cutting into their meals, private time or working hours non-stop over the past few months. As if she didn't know both of their schedules like the freckles on the back of her hand.

Lewis sighed and rubbed at his temples.

'I'm not having this discussion here.'

'We never have this discussion anywhere!'

Mary slammed the spoon onto the table and rose to her feet. She wheeled around to Penny, moving close and pointing a finger directly into the other woman's face. Penny stared at it, her smile unbroken.

'This is all because of you. Why can't you leave us alone?'

Penny stepped back, hand on her heart.

'I don't know what you mean. I only wanted to say thank you to your husband. You seem to be overreacting a little, Mary. Are you feeling well?'

She reached out to Mary, who smacked her hand away and turned back to her husband.

'Lewis, she's doing this on purpose. She hates us! Can't you see what she's doing?'

Lewis was standing now, too. He was smaller than his wife but puffed up his chest like a chicken trying to scare off a predator.

'You are making a scene, Mary.'

'You're siding with her?'

'I'm not siding with anyone. There aren't any sides, Mary.'

Mary began to cry, sniffing loudly and wiping away tears with the corner of a threadbare jumper. Lewis' face crumpled, and he reached out an arm for her, only to be batted away.

'Don't touch me.'

Her voice was stern, but it broke halfway through the sentence. Lewis winced, and tried to reach out for her again. Gentler. His hand brushed her cheek and Mary sobbed loudly, before turning and fleeing from the room. Lewis watched her go, scratching at his head as he looked from the door to Penny, who was now standing much, much closer.

'Go,' said Penny, placing her hand on his shoulder. 'You need to chase after her. Go on.'

Lewis nodded, smiled and ran out of the door after his wife.

Penny counted to thirty, and then sauntered along behind him.

She found Lewis in his bedroom, his head in his hands as he sat on the edge of the bed. He looked broken and small, like a dead insect, its limbs pulled tight towards its centre.

Penny felt sorry for him, really. Though not in the same way she often said aloud to others.

She entered the room, turned and quietly shut the door, locking it behind her with one swift flick of the wrist. It clunked and her stomach dropped.

She ignored the sensation.

At the sound of the click, Lewis' head shot up. His eyes were red and bloodshot, a sight made worse when combined with his usual pallor and roughly shaved stubble.

'Mary?' he said, already halfway to standing before he realised who he was speaking to. He sighed, and sank back onto the bed. It creaked beneath his weight.

'Sorry,' he said. 'I thought she had come back.'

Penny pressed herself up against the door, hands clasped in front of her.

Hips forward.

'What happened?' she asked, softly.

Lewis sniffed.

'She hates me. She said so. Stood here and said it right to my face. I think I've lost her.'

Penny stalked towards him, circling the room like a wolf before sitting next to him on the bed.

She shuffled close, making sure she was near enough that their legs could touch.

'I'm sure that's not true.'

'No. No, it is. I know it. She's never happy anymore. I don't know how to make her happy, Pen.'

'It's not your job to make her happy, Lewis.'

'But she's not happy because of me. It's my fault.'

Penny placed her hand on his leg, and turned her head so that Lewis was looking into her eyes. He smelled cloyingly of sweat and musty fabric, but she managed to force a small smile.

'No, Lewis. It's not your fault. It's hers. You've done everything for her, treated her with more kindness than she deserves, and all she ever does is throw it back in your face.'

She lowered her gaze, but her hand lingered. Her thumb began brushing the fabric of his trousers.

'She doesn't deserve you.'

His hand, dry and bony, reached over and held hers.

'Thank you,' he choked, and then wailed loudly. Penny held him, biting her lip in distaste as he sobbed into her shoulder. She began to rub his back gently. Breathed close to his ear.

She was about to speak when the door handle rattled behind her, followed quickly with a faint knocking.

Her head shot in the direction of the sound, and then desperate to cover herself she laughed and put her hand to her chest.

'That scared me,' she said. 'Shall I see who it is?'

'It's Mary, it has to be.'

Lewis was already starting to stand, but Penny rose to her feet first and pushed him back down onto the bed. He blinked in shock, and she cursed herself for being too hasty.

'You should stay there,' she said. 'Dry your eyes. You don't want her to know you've been crying, do you?'

'But I—'

'Trust me,' she said, and smiled widely. 'I'll take care of it for you. You clean yourself up, and then let me know when you're ready.'

Penny stood and made her way to the door before Lewis could grow a backbone and decide that he would answer it instead. She unlocked it and pulled it open, just slightly, making sure to stand in the gap the open door created.

Mary's face froze when she saw her in the doorway, her neck turning an ugly blotchy pink. Penny casually ran a hand through her hair, and flashed her a coy smile.

'Sorry, could you come back later? We're a little busy right now.'

Mary's mouth opened, about to issue a scathing reply Penny was sure, when Lewis called out from behind her.

'Okay, I'm ready. I'm ready, Pen.'

Penny gave Mary a small shrug, followed by a smirk. Mary started to back away from the door, lips trembling.

She whimpered once and then fled down the corridor.

'Hmm,' said Penny, shutting the door and once again locking it behind her.

She winced and tried to ignore her growing claustrophobia. Hopefully she wouldn't be in here for much longer.

Lewis was standing nearby when she turned around, fidgeting and desperately trying to smooth back his hair.

'I'm sorry, Lewis,' she said. 'It wasn't her.'

Lewis stared.

'That can't be. It had to have been her. Who else could it have been?'

'I'm sorry, Lewis.'

He stumbled back, an amusing imitation of his wife Penny would savour later on.

'She really hates me,' he mumbled. 'She really doesn't love me anymore.'

'There are other women,' said Penny.

Lewis looked at her. His brow furrowed.

Penny reached up and slipped the straps of her dress off her shoulders. The loose material fell to the floor in a puddle of grey fabric.

'Better women,' she said, and smiled.

He'd always loved her smile.

Chapter Seventeen

Murmurs again.

Far away, and then closer.

Muffled, like she was underwater.

There was pressure around her head.

Her shoulders.

Her chest.

Was she dreaming?

Had she made it back to the house, or had that all been a result of the fever? A desperate wish made true by pain and thirst. A dying woman's last daydream.

Perhaps she was still in that field, lying next to her dog and waiting for those creatures to find her.

Her dog.

Nash.

She had forgotten about him. Why had she done that? Where was he now? Was he safe?

Something cold pressed against her forehead, wet and slippery. She shivered.

More murmurs.

Louder this time.

Closer to the surface.

She reached up through the thickness that surrounded her and tried to pull away whatever was pressed against her head, whatever was dripping down her face and pooling above her lips, but something grabbed her hand and held it tight.

Too tight.

Hands around a bird.

It was here.

It had her.

She began to struggle, feathers in her mind, as the murmurs turned to words.

'Hold her down,' said one voice. 'I can't have her kicking at me while I'm trying to take a look.'

'Is it bad?'

'Bad? She should be fucking dead.'

'She's moving again. Penny? Penelope? Can you hear me? You need to keep still.'

Voices. Lots of voices. All around. But where was Nash? She couldn't remember where he went. Was he okay? Was he safe? Did they get him?

'Where's my dog?' said Penny, still pulling against the person holding her arms as she slurred in a hoarse whisper. 'Where is he?'

'Penny, it's okay. You're safe. You're home. Can you hear me? Do you remember where you are?'

'Where's my fucking dog?'

A sigh.

'He's fine. We put him in your old—' The voice, the man, paused. 'He's in your room for now. He was very thin and tired, but he'll be fine. We gave him some food and water. How are you feeling? Do you feel any pain?'

'She'd better be in pain after all the trouble she's caused,' another voice cut in, quieter than the first. 'Not least bringing us another mouth to feed. Under the law we should just dump her back outside.'

'Shut your damn mouth,' Penny gasped, finally gathering the energy to open her eyes.

Everything was blurred initially, like looking at someone through winter-frosted glass. Penny blinked furiously as blobs turned to shapes and shapes became faces. Faces she knew she should recognise, but couldn't.

Three people stood around her, staring down from the sky above. Penny flinched, confused, until she realised she was lying down on a bed. She shuffled onto her elbows and tried to ease herself upright, but the man closest to her gently urged her back down.

'Whoa, try to rest. You're very sick.'

'I'm fine. I've rested. Leave me alone.'

She began to sit up again. The man, seeing this, sighed and placed his arms on her shoulders, firmly holding her in place. She pushed against him, scowling, but she might as well have been pushing against solid rock. She bared her teeth and through the dull pain in her head managed to enjoy the flinch of fear that flashed across the man's face.

'Oh, for God's sake. If she wants to get up, let her. That way we might end up with more food to go around.'

The second man came into view, pink and bald like a newborn rat. Penny turned to him and edged her face as close to his as she could.

'I told you to shut your damn mouth.'

The man sniffed, scowled and folded his arms. He leaned over her until he was close enough that his spittle sprayed against her cheek as he spoke.

'You don't get it, do you? Bringing that mongrel back means we all have just that little bit less time to live, and that's if nothing has followed you back from wherever you decided to run away to.'

'"Run away?" You miserable little—'

'Enough.'

Something sharp pushed itself into Penny's foot and all the breath left her body. Tears swelled and she clung to the bed, shattered fingernails digging deep into the fabric. Her body lurched against the hands holding her still and she screamed silently, praying for air. For the pain to stop.

The pressure against her foot ceased, though the pain remained, and Penny fell back against the bed, gasping.

A woman, hair the colour and texture of wire, peered over the end of the bed. Her face was indifferent, almost bored, and Penny glared at her.

'What did you do to my foot?' she spat.

The woman stepped away from Penny and moved to the wonky cupboard on the other side of the room. She returned with several strips of fabric, and a half-empty bottle of liquid.

'I touched it. I needed to clean away the pus.'

'Liar. You did something. You—'

'I am trying to save your life.'

The bald man snorted.

'Why bother?' he said, rolling his eyes. 'She doesn't appreciate it.'

'You know precisely why we should bother. She's the first

woman we've had who's been able to reproduce in twenty-seven years. Do you want to wait for another twenty-seven? Or do you happen to have a gigantic supply of medical equipment squirreled away somewhere in order for me to investigate this genetic mutation the old-fashioned way?'

'Waiting a few years might not be too bad.'

The woman glared and the man fell still. She turned her gaze to Penny, still pressed to the bed by the kind man beside her.

'Listen to me and listen carefully. Your foot is badly infected and I'm almost certain you have blood poisoning. If you do, there is really not a lot I can do for you. Not with what I have here. We need to clean the wound immediately and keep a very close eye on it. If the worst happens we may need to amputate, but the risks involved with that are just as bad as leaving it be. I don't know what you did to this foot, but the next time you—'

'The next time I'm running for my life, I'll be sure to walk carefully to avoid any injuries.'

The woman turned crimson.

'Be as rude as you like,' she snapped. 'But you are almost certainly dying. And I still need to clean the wound.'

She bent back over the foot and out of Penny's line of sight. Penny leaned as far as she could to the side in order to see what was happening but the pain came again before she could do anything at all. And this time she could scream.

It took what felt like a day of scraping, pushing, oozing and squeezing before the woman had finished. Penny had been given a wad of fabric to bite down on and the musty cloth was all she could taste by the time the woman had bandaged her up.

'All done. I wouldn't move around too much if I were you.'

Penny spat the cloth out onto the floor and gulped at the cup of lukewarm water held to her lips. Liquid ran down her throat and over her chin. She started to cough and the gentle man at her side pulled the cup away before she could choke. Even as she spluttered, her hands reached out for the cup once more.

'We'll be back in a few hours,' the woman said, gathering her things and pushing the bald man out of the room in front of her. 'Keep an eye on her. Make sure she doesn't do anything stupid.'

The door clicked closed. Penny barely noticed.

'How are you feeling?' the remaining man asked, placing the cup on the floor beside him and then perching on the side of the bed.

'Never better, can't you tell?'

The man chuckled. 'You really are like your father.'

Penny glared at her hands. 'I wouldn't really know, would I?'

The man scratched at his head awkwardly. 'Sorry,' he said. 'I guess you wouldn't. Look, the others have asked me to talk to you. Is that okay?'

'About what?'

'The outside.'

Penny looked up.

Frowned.

The man coughed and rubbed his hands together as if he were cold. 'Look,' he said again, 'no one here has ever been outside as far as you have, not really. We've got the grounds and the gardens and most of us have seen a little past the clearing on scouting trips, but that's it. The elders never tell us anything. Me and the other house-dwellers were hoping... Well, you were gone over a week, you must have seen something useful. Found something. Anything.'

His voice was almost seductive and he leaned closer to her, his hand on hers. Penny's jaw clenched.

She wondered how many of those same house-dwellers had thought about her while she was missing. How many of them had wanted to help her before it turned out she might be useful for more than just bearing children.

'Do you remember how they found my father?' she asked.

The man looked away. 'No. No, I wasn't there. I didn't see.'

'They wouldn't tell me, not at first. But I found out.' She waited for the man to look at her, and only then did she continue. 'His chest had caved in entirely, apparently. It was almost the size of his neck. His face was the colour of grapes and that thing was still wrapped around him, like it was hugging him. They had to bury them together.'

The man's face was white.

'You want to know what I know about the outside? What I found out? I know that the only reason this house is safe is because those things don't know we're here. When one spots you, it will chase you until your feet bleed and you are walking on nothing but oozing stumps.'

She leaned forward and the man leaned away from her, his face filled with fear.

Good, she thought. She wanted him to be afraid.

'I know,' Penny continued, 'that they are strong and fast. They don't feel fear, don't even know what that means. You can't ward them off with charms or urban legends. They can climb and run and they never tire. Only the light can distract them, and once that has gone, you have nothing. They will see you, and once they have, they will never stop until they have you. If they knew we were here, we'd already be dead.'

The man stood up and turned away, slowly covering his face with his hands. 'Stop,' he said, his voice hoarse. 'Please, stop. I don't believe it. I can't.'

He crumpled inwards and Penny felt a flicker of shame for upsetting the man. She sighed. 'Believe me or not. I've seen them. I know them.'

'But that can't be true. If you'd seen them, by your own admission you'd be dead!'

'I was lucky.'

'I can't believe it. If any of that were true, we could be putting everyone in danger anytime anybody left the house.'

'You are,' said Penny.

'But our farming, our scavenging, we would have to stop all of it. People would die. The elders wouldn't send us out at such a risk. Besides, why haven't we seen them before now? If they're that smart, why haven't they come?'

'They have.'

'But they never came again!'

'Like I said, they don't know that we're here. We block the light, which means they don't see us.'

'And now?'

Penny frowned. Goosebumps tickled against her arms. 'What do you mean?'

The man rubbed the back of his neck. 'Well,' he said, 'if you've seen them, what if they've followed you? What if you've drawn them here?'

'I haven't.'

'But we don't know that! By running off you could have put us all in danger.'

Penny's head throbbed.

She could taste bile.

'What do you mean, "running off"? Why do you all keep saying that?'

'Penny, Mary told us what happened.'

Icy water trickled down her spine. In her pain and confusion she had briefly forgotten Mary.

'Did she now? And what exactly did she tell you?'

'She told us you both had a heart to heart. That you told her how awful you felt about everything and that you wanted to leave.'

She expected to be filled with rage beyond belief. Instead, Penny laughed. The sound was harsh and bitter, but the laughter was genuine. She wiped a tear from her eye and looked up at the man, the man she had once known but now couldn't remember.

'And you believed her,' she said. A statement, not a question.

'No, but what else were we to think?' The man sighed, and scratched at his scalp through thick, dark hair. 'What happened, Penny? Why did you leave?'

'Where is she?'

'What? Who?'

'Mary. She has my son. Where is she?'

The man stood and stared out of the fogged window, wiping his hand across the glass to see beyond. 'When... you suddenly turned up like you did, you frightened her. She thought you were going to hurt her. We've asked her to stay away from you for a while.'

'She has my son.'

'She took care of him for you. After you… went away. He's been well looked after, I promise. Mary loves the boy dearly.'

'I'll bet she does.'

The man swallowed loudly, and then gently eased Penny back down into the bed. 'Rest, okay? We need you to get better. We've all missed you, you know. I'll bring you some rations later; you've got to be pretty hungry.'

He made to leave the room. As he turned to shut the door, Penny spoke quietly. 'No. Give my rations to the dog. I'll survive.'

The man smiled, said nothing, and then closed the door.

Penny stared at it, deep in thought.

Run away, had she? Like a coward?

Penny couldn't help but smile. She was many things, many awful, cruel things. But Mary, more than anyone, knew that she wasn't a coward.

Maybe she just needed a little reminder.

People came and went from that point on, though Penny barely noticed them.

Snippets she overheard let her know that she had been in the room for less than a day since arriving, though it seemed longer, and that most people thought she would die within the week.

Beneath the scratchy blanket, Penny stretched and twisted her foot, hoping each time she did that those few moments of rest she'd had would help to lessen the pain.

They did not.

In a rage, she threw back the blankets, swinging her legs off the bed. Her feet dangled over the edge, hovering above the wood but never quite touching it.

Penny inched herself closer to the floor. Sweat stung her eyes and she blinked frantically, gasping for breath that never seemed to fully reach her lungs.

She had walked through this pain before. She had run, damn it. Why couldn't she take that first step?

Her foot brushed itself against the wood. In shock, her body instinctively lurched away. Penny fell back onto the bed, gulping air and shivering.

She had felt nothing, but the anticipation of pain was more than she could bear. Penny bit down on the blanket and screamed until the sound hummed in her mind. She spat out the fabric, grabbed the cup of water balancing on the crooked bedside cabinet and threw it across the room.

'Stupid foot! Stupid house! Stupid! Stupid!'

The cup bounced along the floor but did not smash.

She couldn't even do that right.

Penny curled into a tight ball, knees against her chest, and hid her face beneath the blanket so that nobody could see her cry.

Time passed and the light in the room faded from a dim cream to a fuzzy grey.

Penny's eyes ached and her throat was sore from the sobs she kept within. Her stomach gurgled and cramped. Penny could feel bubble-like movement when she pressed her fingers against her stomach but she would rather starve than call out and ask for something to eat.

Initially.

Once the room began to spin, she started to count back the days, trying to remember the last time she ate anything other than the handfuls of berries she'd stopped to grab on her way up the hill.

She couldn't.

Her shoulders sagged in defeat and she began to clear her throat in order to call out when she heard the door begin to creak open.

Penny pushed her face deeper into the mattress.

Nobody could see her like this. What would they think?

'Are you awake?'

A whisper, as if the person did not want to be heard.

Penny stiffened.

'Hello?' came the voice again. Quiet, nervous.

Female.

Penny knew that voice.

She would always know that voice.

The door clicked closed and Penny held her breath, not wanting to give herself away if Mary had entered.

Had she entered?

There was a moment of silence and Penny had almost convinced herself that Mary had lost her courage until she heard the sound of a chair being dragged away from the bed. Penny dug her hands into the mattress until her fingernails ached.

She squeezed.

Mary said nothing but Penny could hear her heavy breathing, a panicked pant slowly becoming a slow, shuddering sigh.

'I can't say I'm sorry,' she said finally, almost under her breath. 'I can't. I wouldn't mean it. I'm not sorry, not even a little. I just… I never thought… I've never been scared like that. When I saw you in the doorway, I thought you were going to kill me.'

She stopped.

Took another deep breath.

'You probably were going to kill me, weren't you? Would have, if you hadn't been sick. I should have known you'd come back. You never seemed like you were completely finished, not even after Lewis. Of course you would come back. God, one mistake. I made one mistake.'

Beneath the blanket Penny began biting the inside of her cheek, hoping the pain would stop her from shouting out.

A *mistake*?

When Mary next spoke, her voice trembled.

'You've spent your whole life trying to ruin mine. Do you think that I don't regret what happened? That I don't think about it every single day? See it when I close my eyes? He meant a lot to me too. You know that. Knew that, anyway.' She sniffed, and Penny almost thought she sounded sincere.

Almost.

'I've lost everyone. Everything I have ever loved. When I sent you away, I thought that would be it. You were finally gone, and I had something in my life to make it worth living again. I was happy. And now you've come back to take him from me too.'

Mary's voice cracked.

Was she crying?

Why was she crying?

'You're the devil.'

Penny closed her eyes. There was a knot in her chest, like a hand gripping her heart, and her cheeks burned. A quiet voice began to murmur in the back of her mind.

You've done enough.

She's sorry.

She tried to kill you, shouted another voice, her voice. Her rage.

She stole everyone first.

She deserves everything.

The chair crashed against the wooden floor and something snapped loudly.

'You're the devil,' said Mary again, almost sounding surprised. More confident. Her voice rose. 'You're the devil. And you should have died in the forest like your coward of a father.'

The door slammed.

Footsteps receded, fading into nothing.

Penny stared blankly, tears creeping into her eyes. She blinked and allowed them to fall.

The knot in her chest unravelled and fell to the pit of her stomach.

Penny rolled onto her back and peeled the blanket off her skin.

The room came into view, pale like mist at first, the dull metal of the bed frame glinting as the moonlight fell upon it. She blinked, turned to the window. They had forgotten to cover it.

Oh well. That didn't matter now.

She swung her legs until they were off the bed.

She sat up.

Placed her feet on the cool, hard floor.

Her injured foot exploded in pain.

Penny didn't notice.

It was as if she were underwater again. Her body was slow and hard to control, her limbs heavy. Her breathing was laboured and wet. She could barely think and each step towards the door felt like someone hammering a nail deep into the arch of her foot.

In the corner of the room, a wooden chair lay broken on the

floor, one leg almost completely severed from the rest. Penny limped over to it and snapped it off entirely.

It wasn't heavy, but Penny didn't mind.

In fact, she looked forward to having to put in the extra effort.

She ran a finger down the length of the leg, feeling the rough texture beneath her skin, and then sluggishly made her way out of the room.

The corridor was empty.

Dark.

Penny looked from left to right, scanning the shadows for the faintest movement.

There was a rustle to her left.

A soft thud.

Penny moved without hesitation, one hand against the wall for balance, the other wrapped around the chair leg.

She could smell dust and old paper, stale books.

She was near the library.

Was that where Mary had gone?

Penny could remember a rainy afternoon in the library, rolling thunder and hushed voices. Her son on her lap, sleeping. Warm. Close. His heartbeat against hers. Her father had read to her. Had she ever read to her son? She couldn't remember.

Penny stopped outside the library door.

Voices.

Movement.

She pushed against the door and it slammed against the wall.

Warm light flickered.

A dog barked.

She blinked, adjusting to the light as a weight pushed against her, soft fur brushing against her exposed legs.

She smiled.

'Hey boy, hey.'

Nash pushed his face against her, whining quietly, tail wagging. Penny leaned over and scratched at his face. He circled her, panting, and then ran towards the light.

A small boy stood at the far end of the room, balanced beside a fireplace with a book in his hands. The book fell to the ground with a thunk.

The boy clasped his hands together. Tucked his shoulders in.

His eyes were wide.

Frightened.

Why was he frightened?

Penny's chest began to ache, a pain stronger than anything she had experienced over the past week. She crouched down until she was on her knees, and her face was level with his.

'I'm home, baby. I'm here. I'm home.'

The boy took a step backward. He was pale. Trembling.

'It's me,' Penny said. 'It's Mama.'

She reached out for him, a single arm extended.

He stepped backward again.

Nash ran over to him, sniffing at the boy's face, so close in height to his own. The boy patted the dog's head gently. His eyes grew warm. Penny couldn't remember him ever looking at her like that. Did he look at Mary like that?

'Do you like him?' Penny asked the boy.

He nodded, but would not look at her.

'His name is Nash. You can look after him, if you like. Would you like that?'

He nodded again and Penny sighed in relief.

'I'm glad. We can keep him in our room. Won't that be fun? He can keep you company while I'm doing my chores. That way you won't be lonely.'

The boy looked up at her.

His eyes filled with tears.

'I don't want to go.'

'What?'

'I don't want to go. I don't want to. Aunty said I could stay with her. Why can't I stay with her?'

'Aunty?'

The boy said nothing.

'Who is Aunty?'

Nothing.

She rose to her feet.

'Mary? Are you talking about Mary?'

Nothing. Why the hell wasn't he answering her?

Penny dragged herself forward, eyes flashing.

'For God's sake, answer me you stupid little boy!'

The boy whimpered.

His eyes were a deep blue in the candle light. A twilight sky. Like her father's.

Penny faltered, lowering the arms she had already extended to grab the boy. She tried to apologise, but the words came out choked and strained. By the time she could speak, the boy had fled from the room, taking Nash with him.

Penny stood beside the fire, a thousand agonising thoughts buzzing in her mind.

Mary had poisoned the boy against her.

Penny had frightened the boy.

Mary had taken everything.

A mistake. Just a mistake.

She had tried to kill her.

Her father.

It was all Mary's fault.

Lewis. Penny had taken Lewis.

She had deserved it.

Not her fault.

All her fault.

The boy.

Her boy.

Her father.

Mary.

The log house.

Penny wiped her eyes. Her grip tightened against the wooden chair leg. Slowly, she made her way out of the room.

She turned right, back towards the way she came. Past the room she had awoken in. Towards the stairs.

Penny paid no attention to anything around her. There was no longer any need to search through the house. It had been stupid to search in the first place.

There was only one place Mary would be.

Penny stepped out into the night air and breathed in the frosty darkness until her throat burned with the cold. The door shut loudly behind her, but that didn't matter. Nobody would be stupid enough to follow her into the dark.

She briefly checked for any trace of light that might have sneaked its way out alongside her and then made her way onto the frozen grass. She walked slowly, savouring the moonlight as its brightness dimmed in and out of the clouds wrapped around it. The clouds that grabbed it with smoky fingers.

Grabbed it.

Penny shuddered.

Her grip on the chair leg tightened as she rounded the corner of the house.

At the edge of the forest, crumbling into the dirt and nearly hidden by the thick shadows of the trees, was a small wooden shed. Its door hung open, like a broken jaw, allowing a glimpse of the darkness within.

She remembered that darkness. It followed her everywhere.

The log house, they called it, though nobody had gone near it since she had been a child. It had once been used as a store for firewood, to keep it dry throughout the winter months, though it was barely large enough to hold a month's supply at a time. She remembered her father travelling out into the forest in order to top it up every few months.

She remembered the door swinging shut.

She remembered the screaming.

A splinter of wood pushed into her palm and Penny limped onward.

Mary was standing beside the log house, hair glinting in the moonlight as she stared into its depths. Her thoughts had always been obvious to Penny, clear as glass. After that scene in the bedroom, all those awful memories dragged to the surface, there was no way Mary would have been anywhere else. Mary would want to think back to the start of everything, run through everything to ensure she had done everything *right*. Everything *good*. But Mary had never been one for imagination. She would need to physically be near the log house to picture it.

That suited Penny fine.

Penny moved closer. Mary's back was to the main house, and to Penny. It would be easy from where she was standing to creep up behind her, just one swing would be all it would take, and then she'd be gone.

Just like Mary had done to her.

No.

Penny wasn't like her.

She wasn't a coward.

She wanted to look into the woman's eyes as she swung the wooden chair leg at her. She wanted Mary to see her coming, wanted to see the expression on her face as she realised what was happening. What was about to happen.

The trees rustled around her like a chorus of spirits goading her towards her target.

Penny kept moving until she was directly behind her prey. She leaned over, placing her mouth next to Mary's ear.

She exhaled.

Mary shrieked, spinning around wildly. As she did so, Penny pushed her into the wall of the little wooden shed with her chair leg. Mary crashed against it, seemingly too frightened to wince at the impact.

Penny raised the leg until it was pressed hard against Mary's throat.

Mary started to gasp for air.

'I'm really glad we're meeting here,' Penny spat. 'I couldn't dream of anywhere better.'

Then Penny started to push.

Before #6

It had snowed the evening before for the first time since she had been born.

The silence of it all had astounded her. It was unlike anything she had ever seen, a calmness like the still water of a clear pond. Gentle, beautiful and yet peculiar and eerie.

Penny stood in the doorway to the house, not daring to take that first step onto the strange blanket of white. Mary, just barely eighteen, crouched beside the little girl and smiled.

'What's the matter?' she asked. 'Don't you want to play in the snow?'

'It looks weird.'

'It's fun. Look.' Mary turned and pointed to a figure at the end of the garden, half-hidden in the forest's edge. 'There's your father. He doesn't mind the snow.'

Penny frowned and squinted into the distance.

A tall man swung an axe at a felled tree, hacking it into pieces and kicking the chucks into a pile. When the pile reached a certain height, the man tossed the pieces into the little wooden building beside him, the log house, and then started again.

Penny watched her father from the house.

'Dad!' she called.

No reply.

'He can't hear you,' Mary said, smiling just a little. 'You'll have to get closer.'

Penny clenched her little fists, glowered, and then rushed out onto the snow.

The wetness creeped into her thin fabric shoes instantly, and she gasped at the sensation. She curled her toes until she wobbled as she walked, and ignored the sound of Mary laughing behind her.

She reached a large stone halfway across the garden and hopped onto it.

'Dad!'

This time the man stopped. He threw down his axe, wiped his brow with a ragged sleeve and turned towards her. He squinted and smiled, waving over his head.

Penny returned the wave, smiling widely herself.

She jumped off the rock and ran to her father, jumping at him with arms outstretched. The man grabbed Penny around the waist, spinning her in a circle at a dizzying speed, and causing her legs to swing through the air behind her.

Penny laughed, breathless and stomach aching, as he placed her back onto the frozen ground.

'And what are you doing out here? I thought you didn't like the cold.'

'Mary wanted to show me the snow.'

'Did she now?' the man said, winking at Mary.

'How is it going, Mr Thomas?' she asked, placing a gentle hand on Penny's head. He shrugged. Penny wriggled out of Mary's grasp and stuck out her tongue.

'I'd like to say it's the same as it always is this time of year, but this snow has not done us any favours. Most of the trees are far too damp for firewood, but if the snow holds off we might be able to dry the logs enough for us to use them.'

He paused.

'Pen.'

Penny jumped and sheepishly moved away from the door of the log house.

'I just wanted to look.'

'I know. It's not safe, baby. The door's still broken. You don't want to be stuck inside, do you?'

Penny shook her head, eyes to the ground and face burning.

'Sorry,' she said.

Mary cleared her throat.

'Mr Thomas, why don't you take a break and play with us?'

Penny's father put his hand on his waist and pursed his lips together.

'Hmm. Is that what you want me to do, Pen?'

She nodded eagerly, thankful to have got off as lightly as she had.

Her father rubbed his chin, scratching at his stubble with rough fingers covered in mud.

'Well, I don't know. I've got a lot of work to do. I mean, just look at all that over there.'

He pointed behind her, and Penny turned staring into the forest. She frowned. There wasn't anything there.

'Dad, I don't see—'

Something cold smacked the back of her head, and then dripped down the collar of her jumper. Penny shrieked, brushing away the snow that was sliding down her neck as she spun back around to glare at her father. The man opened his mouth wide in exaggerated shock, and then pointed at Mary.

Penny glowered at the older girl and crouched in the snow, gathering a ball of it into her numb, pink hands. Mary ran, screaming and laughing, and fell onto the ground. Penny stood over her, throwing lumps of snow.

'No, stop! Stop!' Mary shouted, breathless from the laughter. 'I give up.'

Penny grinned and looked over at her father.

'Dad, I won. Look, Dad!'

Her smile faded.

Her father wasn't facing her, but was staring intently into the forest.

'Dad? What's wrong?'

Her father looked from the line of trees then back to the two girls. His eyebrows were furrowed and deep angry lines, the kind Penny only saw when he was really angry, were carved into his forehead.

'Nothing,' he said. 'It's nothing. I thought I saw something.'

The girls stood and made their way back to him. Mary grabbed Penny's hand and held it tight.

A flock of birds shot out from the forest in front of them, rushing towards the pink-cream sky. Snowdrifts fell from the trees, disturbed by the flapping of wings, and then crumbled to the ground in muffled thumps. Penny's father squinted into the forest again.

'What is it, Mr Thomas?'

He said nothing, but held a single finger to his lips.

Mary squeezed Penny's hand.

Something was wrong.

She stared out towards the forest.

Snow swirled in the air, creating patterns that made her dizzy. But beyond the snow there was something else.

Something moving.

What was that?

Penny's father took a step backward, snow crunching. He winced.

'Mary, take Penny inside. Warn the elders.'

'What's wrong? What's happening? Is it—'

'You need to go. I'll distract it while you run. Lock the door behind you.'

'But what about you?'

Penny's father smiled at them grimly.

'I'll lock myself in the log house. It's closer. Safe. You need to go.'

A rattling echoed out from behind the trees. A distorted voice that cut through the silence. Penny looked from Mary to her father.

Their faces were pale.

Terrified.

'Move!'

The girls ran.

Mary half-dragged Penny to the house; her little feet were unable to keep up with the older girl.

'Not much farther,' Mary panted. 'Almost there. Not much farther.'

The beating of Penny's heart was overwhelming her ears so much that she couldn't hear her father's footsteps behind her. She looked over her shoulder, wanting to see his face, wanting to see him reassure her with his warm smile.

He was not behind her.

Penny skidded to a stop, digging her feet into the snow.

Where was he?

Where had he gone?

'Penny, come on!'

'I don't see him. Mary, I don't see him. Where's my dad?'

'He's heading to the log house. Penny, please. You need to move.' Mary tugged at her hand, but Penny held firm, scanning the trees.

Movement.

Yes, there he was.

Axe in hand.

His back to her.

Heading into the forest.

Away from the log house.

Penny wailed, straining against Mary's grip.

'Let go,' she cried. 'He's going the wrong way. Let go. Let go!'

Mary pulled at her, dragging her towards the house.

Her father disappeared behind a tree.

Breathless and without thinking she turned and bit down on Mary's hand.

The girl screamed and her grip loosened.

Penny pulled her hand away and ran towards the forest.

Snow flew as Penny raced towards her father. She tried to call out to him, wanting to scream for him to stop, but her chest burned and she could barely whisper his name. She watched as her father came into view, and raised the axe high above his head.

There was something else there. Something smiling, staggering in the snow.

She screamed.

Footsteps beside her. Two arms wrapped around her waist, lifting her off the ground. Penny writhed in Mary's arms, kicking out, powerless. She was thrown into the log house, and Mary tumbled in behind her. They fell into a mountain of wood, knocking it and causing the logs to roll to the floor.

Penny crawled over Mary, who grabbed her tightly by the ankle before she could get away.

Penny was slammed into the floor.

She looked up.

In front of her was a small patch of sunlight, cast onto the ground by the open doorway.

An area of light that was slowly, and steadily, getting smaller.

Penny wailed, but too late. The door slammed shut, and the light vanished.

Darkness.

The sound of breathing and the faint whisper of wind.

Penny blinked, her eyes throbbing as tears began to fall.

'No,' she whimpered. 'No, no, no.'

She staggered forward blindly, hands extended. The pads of her fingers brushed wood, and she searched the darkness for a door handle she knew didn't exist.

'Mary. Mary, you have to open the door.'

'I can't.'

'But my dad is outside. He's still out there. We have to let him in. He said he'd be coming here. You need to open the door or he can't come in.'

Mary said nothing.

'Mary,' said Penny, voice cracking. 'Please. Open the door.'

'I'm sorry, Penny. I'm really sorry.'

'Mary, you need to open the door.'

There was a crash against the door from outside, followed by a frantic knocking. Penny jumped and then cried out, tears streaming down her face. She slammed her hands against the door as the man on the other side called her name.

Screamed it.

'Mary!' Penny shrieked.

'It's locked.'

'Mary, please. We have to help him. We have to.'

'I can't do anything!'

The knocking stopped.

In its stead Penny could hear something sigh, and then the faint sound of choking.

Breath leaving a body.

A hand gripped her shoulder and Penny slapped it away.

The choking grew quieter.

Softer.

And then, with a final rattle, stopped completely.

The world was still once more.

Penny could hear her own breathing echoing in her head. Mary sniffed in the corner.

'I'm sorry,' she said. 'I just wanted to save you. I didn't mean to lock the door. I'm sorry.'

Hot tears dripped onto Penny's clenched hand like rain.

'Penny, I'm sorry.'

Penny touched the wooden door, picturing her father's smile.

'You will be.'

Chapter Eighteen

Mary wheezed, her hands clawing desperately at the wooden chair leg as Penny pushed it harder against her throat. Flapping wildly.

Like a bird.

'Please…' she said, gasping for breath. Reaching out.

It was such a shame they were out here in the dark. Penny would have liked to see her face turn purple.

Like her husband's had.

'Please…' Mary said again.

'Oh, I can't,' Penny hissed.

'Please…'

'I'm so sorry. I *can't.*'

Penny dragged out the words, almost singing them. She enjoyed the taste of the syllables on her tongue and she savoured the sound of them. Mary's chokes were wet, as if she were drowning.

Penny liked that very much.

'You deserve this,' she said. 'You deserve all of this.'

'I'm… I'm…'

'Sorry? I've heard that before. If you wanted to steal my son from me, you should at least have had the guts to kill me yourself.'

'You stole… my—'

Penny pushed harder. Mary slapped at Penny's arm, her fingernails scratching at her skin. She was starting to make a delicious gurgling noise as she tried to breathe.

'I'd be very quiet if I were you. You don't want to be wasting all that lovely air.'

Mary wrapped her hands around Penny's wrists, trying to push the chair leg away from her throat, but Penny had found a hidden pool of strength. Sweat ran down her neck and her legs trembled, but her arms couldn't be moved.

Mary's eyes rolled back and then closed.

Something brushed gently against Penny's heel. She hissed,

immediately knowing what was about to happen, but not able to move fast enough to prevent it.

Mary stomped down on Penny's injured foot.

Once.

Twice.

Hard.

Penny shrieked, dark spots fluttering into her vision as something burst under the pressure. She dropped the wooden leg, and fell to the floor. The world lurched around her. Hot liquid oozed from her wound and the smell of it entwined with the pain as her stomach churned.

She heaved.

Threw up on the grass.

Penny wiped her mouth and looked up, acid burning her nostrils, just in time to see Mary on her knees. Crawling away from her.

'No!' Penny screamed, forgetting the pain and diving onto the woman.

Mary thrashed as Penny pinned her to the earth.

'I have nothing left!' Mary wheezed. 'Haven't you ruined my life enough?'

Penny fought to reach her throat.

'Not even close,' she spat. 'Not before you tried to kill me, and definitely not now.'

'What other choice did I have? I had to send you away. I had to get rid of you. You don't understand, do you? You are poison. You're a devil. You destroy everything and everyone around you. The boy would have been miserable with you. Don't you know how much you frighten him? You would have ruined his life. You are nothing but spite.'

'If I *want* to ruin his life, if I *want* to make him stand on his head like a lunatic or break every bone in his little body, I will.' Penny leaned close, inches away from Mary's face. 'I am his mother. He belongs to *me*. He is not your son.'

'He should have been!' Mary shrieked, pushing Penny off and scrambling to her feet. Penny chased after her and reached out, aiming for Mary's hair but coming short and instead grabbing a handful of her shirt. They struggled together, evenly matched, glaring at each other in the dark. 'Did you even think about your son when you were in that forest?'

'Of course I did.'

Mary scoffed.

'No, you didn't. Of course you didn't. You thought about me, didn't you? About having him stolen from you, like a child losing a toy. Did you ever miss him? Did you ever think about wanting to hold him? Wanting to tuck him in?'

'Of course I did,' Penny said again, but this time less certain.

She had thought about all those things. Hadn't she?

Mary smirked. 'You're not a mother. You're just a dirty, lying whore.'

'Shut your damn—'

Arm raised ready to strike, Penny stopped.

Somewhere behind her, somewhere in the night, there had been a noise. Penny scanned around, her eyes rolling in their sockets. She didn't dare move her head.

Mary frowned. 'What are you—'

'Quiet,' Penny hissed.

The sound came again. A snap and a rustle of grass.

Something was moving towards them.

A flicker of light.

Candle light.

Penny's legs turned to water.

'Aunty?' came a small little voice.

'Oh God.'

'Mama?'

The child stepped out from behind the log house, stubby candle wobbling in his small, trembling hands.

'Aunty? I heard you cry. Why are you crying?'

He stepped closer to them and the candle flickered.

The moisture left Penny's mouth and her mind grew blank. She watched as Mary stood and ran to the boy, holding his face in her hands.

'What are you doing out here? It's not safe. You need to go back inside.'

The candle flickered again.

Penny regained control of her body.

She wailed and lunged at the boy, crushing the flame with her palm and throwing the candle into the trees.

'What are you doing?' Mary yelled, ripping Penny away from the child. Penny grabbed her and covered her mouth.

Silence.

No wind.

No trees.

Only a faint rustling.

Distant rattling.

Dead lungs.

'Haaaa.'

Slowly, Penny lowered her hand.

'Don't move,' she whispered. 'Don't speak, just stay calm. It might not have seen the light. It might not see us. We have to stay still.'

Mary looked around, then back at Penny. She pulled the boy close to her. 'I didn't hear anything.'

'Quiet!'

'You think you're really funny, don't you? Here of all places. You're disgusting. There are no creatures here, there haven't been for years.'

'Mary, please. We have to be quiet. We have to get back to the house. Please.'

Mary, please. Open the door.

Mary shook her head. She put her hand in her pocket.

'What are you doing?' Penny whispered.

Mary said nothing. Instead she pulled out a small box from her pocket, barely the length of a finger. She shook it at Penny and the box rattled.

'You are nothing but a liar, and I can prove it.'

Realisation hit Penny in the gut.

'Mary, don't—'

Her plea came too late. There was a scratch, a match, and then a flame.

Mary's face flickered in the orange light, shadows dancing on her face. She smiled, triumphantly.

'See?' she said, looking at the boy, 'Your mother is just a big, dirty—'

Another snap. This time closer.

Something white moved beyond the trees, small and thin. Large eyes refracted green predatory light.

Mary dropped the box.

The match flickered once and was gone.

'Run,' Penny whispered.

Mary did not move.

The boy started to cry.

'Run!'

Penny grabbed her son, so much smaller than she remembered, and began to drag him to the house. She limped and grunted, her speed slowing with every step, but never stopping. She could never stop.

There was another set of footsteps following behind.

Mary or the creature, it didn't matter.

She couldn't look back.

Run.

Just run.

Move the boy.

Save the boy.

She breathed heavily, every muscle straining.

'Mama,' the boy cried. 'I'm scared. I'm scared.'

The house loomed ahead.

Doors.

Locks.

If they could get inside, they would be safe. He would be safe. She only had to get him inside.

Foot collided with rock.

Pressure.

Pain.

The sky was the floor, her foot was liquid fire and she rolled into the dirt.

Her head hit the ground, bounced.

Her consciousness began to fade.

In and out.

A warm hand grabbed hers and began to pull.

Her vision was a tornado, she was unable to focus on anything before it spun away, but the voice came clear to her.

'Come on,' said Mary. 'Come on, get up, come on.'

Why was she helping her? Penny didn't understand. There was no reason for her to be helping.

The rattling was louder.

Closer.

It throbbed in her head.

It would be on her soon.

Mary began to pull frantically. Like she had done when she had been just a child.

Penny stumbled to her feet. Swayed.

The house was so far.

Too far.

She would never make it.

'Get away from me,' Penny croaked.

Mary pulled again.

'Move. Come on. Please.'

Penny grabbed her son by his shoulders and shoved him towards Mary.

'Go to the house.'

'What?'

'I can't run that far. Go to the house!'

Mary gripped the boy.

Opened her mouth to speak.

Winced.

Ran.

Penny watched them go.

Took a deep breath.

Turned around.

Something was dragging itself out of the forest, its limbs bent and twisted, as if it had fallen and rolled down a large, rocky hill.

A pale broken spider.

Still alive.

How was it still alive?

Olivia's monster paused. Large black eyes moved slowly from left to right.

Its head twitched. Its smile stretched wider.

The thing let out a long, slow breath, rose to its feet and then started to run.

At her.

To her.

Penny closed her eyes and breathed deeply.

It was better this way.

Once it had her, it would wrap its arms around her and then it would never move again.

Wind rushed past her ear.

She turned.

The creature had shot past Penny without a second thought.

It did not see her.

Penny exhaled and followed the creature with her eyes. It was running to the house. To Mary.

To her son.

'No!'

She shouted.

She screamed.

'Here! Come here!'

The creature smiled.

They were not near the house.

Too slow.

They wouldn't make it.

She'd led it here. She'd killed them. This was all her fault. Everything had always been her fault.

Her son. Her child. Robin. His name was Robin. His face in her mind, candle lit, so much like her father's.

Penny clenched her fist.

She could do something. She could draw it to her. Save them.

The candle.

The matches.

The light.

Penny ran.

She ran and ran.

Breathed and ran, gasped and stumbled and fell, grasped and crawled. *They have to be here somewhere. Where?* She could hear it. Mary, her son, they wouldn't make it. She needed the matches *now*.

Box.

Match.

Shaking fingers.

Please.

Please, light.

Please.

A scratch.

A flame.

A pause.

Penny could feel each bead of sweat on her body, every prickle across her skin.

She listened to her breathing, to her chest rise and fall, and watched as the creature, so close to its prey, turned slowly towards the light.

Penny stepped backward.

'Come here,' she mumbled. 'Follow the light. Come to me.'

She was shaking. Must have been the cold.

Another step.

Her hand shot about in the darkness behind her. It hit cold, damp wood.

The creature was coming.

Smiling.

She remembered her son smiling. A real smile. Teeth missing. Cheeks rosy. A warm smile.

Penny's feet moved from dirt to wood.

The door was beside her, a large stone keeping it in place.

Can't have it lock again.

Dangerous, Pen.
Stay away.
It was so close.
So close.
Were they inside yet?
Heat against her fingers.
Had they made it?
Didn't matter.
Not now.
She kicked the stone.
Dropped the match.
Closed her eyes.
Robin's smile.
Stretched.
Her father's hands.
Around her throat.
Pressure.
Smiles.
Pain.
Darkness.
And the sound of a door slamming shut.

Acknowledgements

Thank you first of all to my family, who allowed me to grow up weird even after I started writing horrific stories for my primary school library. Though you probably should have checked the content before I put one on the shelves. That was a lot of blood in a story for eight year olds.

Thank you to everyone who read drafts and excerpts of *The Log House* and did not immediately follow up with: 'But you have a real job too, right?'

Thank you to my editors – Claire, Molly and Deborah – for helping me to shape my novel into something I could be proud of.

Thank you to Unbound and Xander, who gave me this chance in the first place, and to all the lovely Unbound authors who lifted my spirits when I was feeling low.

Finally, thank you (yes, you) for your support.

You are incredible, and wonderful and a little bit strange.

You know that, right?

Patrons

Alys Earl
Keith Gale
Tim Guthat
Merv Hart
Sam Haysom
Georgia Heavens
Sandy Herbert
E O Higgins
Kris Holt
Shona Kinsella
C Pepp
Justin Ricks
Noomi Spook
Carol Wilshire
Joshua Winning
horror-writers.net